... When Geoffrey's soft lips touched her hand, goose-bumps rippled up her arm and down to her toes. Kate fought to keep from blushing.

The glance that met hers, when she finally looked up, was warm and gentle. Kate felt as if his eyes had touched her soul. Had she known him for a lifetime—or only a few moments?

"You'll see plenty of me, for I am a frequent customer and caller." Geoffrey's hand still held hers, and his eyes sparkled.

Kate knew the thrill of feeling precious to a man. *Our hearts agree!* her mind exclaimed. *Why else would he have looked that way?*

Watching Geoffrey turn reluctantly to his friends, she thought of the heroes from her books. *None is as fine as he: handsome, charming, and wealthy. What more could a girl ask for? I've finally met the man of my dreams.*

BY Barbara A. Masci:

Forbidden Legacy
Captured Heart
Stolen Heritage
Dangerous Illusions

DANGEROUS ILLUSIONS

BARBARA A·MASCI

Fleming H. Revell Company
Tarrytown, New York

Scripture quotations in this volume are from the King James Version of the Bible.

Library of Congress Cataloging-in-Publication Data

Masci, Barbara A.
    Dangerous illusions / Barbara A. Masci.
        p.   cm.
    ISBN 0-8007-5393-3
    I. Title.
PS3563.A7817D36   1991
813'.54—dc20   90-26219
                                                                    CIP

Copyright © 1991 by Barbara A. Masci
Published by the Fleming H. Revell Company
Tarrytown, New York
Printed in the United States of America

TO my parents, Genevieve and
Theodore Thomas:
"And that from a child thou hast
known the holy scriptures, which are
able to make thee wise unto salvation
through faith which is in Christ Jesus."

2 Timothy 3:15

DANGEROUS ILLUSIONS

1

*A*fter frantically brushing the dust from the sleeves and bodice of her gray traveling dress, the young woman clapped her white-gloved hands together to rid them of the grit. As the stagecoach squeaked toward the livery, she fought down a desire to call it back. The last familiar sight—part of her travels since she'd boarded it in Kansas City—disappeared behind the little red train station just as she leaned forward, one hand half raised to beckon to the driver.

Absently tucking her stray brown curls into her bonnet, Kate Hunter realized her hair was already damp with perspiration and the loose locks curled tightly about her face. No morning had ever been this hot in Chicago.

Looking about in wonder, Kate sighed. "So this is Hays City, Kansas." Shiny rails of the newly laid train tracks glistened in the early morning sun; a man on the stage had promised that by spring the Kansas Pacific Railroad would run right through Hays.

Kate climbed up a wobbly step, onto the wooden sidewalk, shaded her eyes with her hands, and read a crowd of signs, announcing: CABLE AND WYATT OUTFITTING STORE; DALTON'S SALOON AND FARO HOUSE; THE PERTY HOTEL; WHITE'S BARBER SHOP; M. E. JOYCE, JUSTICE OF THE PEACE. Various other businesses littered the street. To the north lay a courthouse square, complete with sheriff's office and jail.

In the midst of such a crowd she could not perceive one human form.

Kate tapped one high, laced boot on the sidewalk nervously. The school-district agent had promised that someone would meet her. Should she remain there on the sidewalk or venture along the street?

Before she had time to answer her own question three figures popped out of one of the buildings and walked swiftly toward her. Kate breathed deeply and prayed silently, *O Lord, please let that be someone sent to meet me.*

As they approached she noticed that the large figure practically pushed the two smaller forms. Soon she could distinguish two small, red-headed boys who made her think she was seeing double and a tall, sturdy woman, her hand clutching two small shoulders almost painfully.

The woman nodded curtly and asked, "Are you the new teacher?"

Kate nodded shyly and smiled. "I'm Katherine Hunter, but everyone calls me Kate. Did the school-district agent send you to meet me?"

"Yes. My name is Margo Dutton," she stated forthrightly. "And this is Carl and Earl." She pushed each petrified boy forward respectively. As the freshly scrubbed, identical faces gazed up at her, Kate wondered, *How will I ever tell them apart?*

"Twins?" she asked their blond-haired mother.

"Yes, they'll be ten years old in October. They can't wait for school to start." She prodded her boys with her hand, gently this time. "Can you, boys?"

Both nodded, and Kate noted that beneath the freckles their cheeks became almost as red as their heads.

"Is the schoolhouse far?" she asked, looking up and down the street paved with buffalo sod.

"We don't have a schoolhouse, yet . . . ," Margo began.

"But the agent said. . . ." Kate could barely contain her surprise and anger.

Margo turned her boys around and said cheerfully, "Let's go home and talk."

"H-home?" Kate asked, bewildered.

"Yes, you'll stay first in our home. Didn't O'Brien tell you that you'd be boarding around?"

"Boarding around?" Kate stopped, frozen to the wooden walk. "What does that mean?"

Margo Dutton threw back her head in laughter. "It's not half as bad as it sounds, and it'll sound even better in my kitchen, over a hot cup of tea."

With a helpless shrug Kate silently followed Margo down the walk and through the front door of the store under the sign THE DUTTON SWEET SHOP.

Even in her agitation Kate appreciated the smell of freshly baked bread, pies, and cakes. What a delightful place to live! Shelves along the side and back walls of the shop displayed the baked goods and homemade candies. Kate's empty stomach lurched; she hadn't eaten today.

A thin, white-aproned man smiled warmly from behind the counter.

"Miss Kate Hunter, I'd like you to meet my husband, Mr. Elmer Dutton."

Elmer stretched out a clean, firm hand, and Kate gladly

accepted it. "How do you do, Mr. Dutton?" She immediately liked this gentle man with twinkling, kind eyes. His hair, in contrast to his wife's, gleamed black as coal—except the top, where a bald spot shone through.

Margo pushed Kate through a back door and asked over her shoulder, "Mind the store and the twins for about an hour, Mr. Dutton?"

"Sure, take your time," he answered. "Nice meeting you, Miss Hunter."

She nodded, felt Margo's gentle push, and soon found herself sitting at a wooden table in a comfortable kitchen that made her momentarily homesick.

As Margo poured tea into delicate china cups Kate studied her. Her hostess was lofty, broad, and muscular, reminding Kate of the Grecian statues she'd seen in books: beautiful but full-bodied and strong.

Margo's hair reminded Kate of butter, and she wore the tresses braided and wound about her head. A complexion like milk and honey complemented eyes as blue as the sky on the clearest day. Only the merest wrinkles at her eyes denoted her age and the frequency of her smiles.

Before joining Kate, Margo slapped a pan of honey buns, fresh from the large oven, onto the table. "They're best hot." She winked.

"They look luscious, and I'm so very hungry," Kate admitted.

Margo patted Kate's hand. "While they cool a bit, let me explain away some of your worries." She slid into the kitchen chair across from Kate and smiled. "First of all, boarding around isn't so terrible. I think it will be fun." Margo slipped a flat utensil under each honey bun and placed them on an oval platter that matched the china cups. "We arranged for our last teacher to live with a different district family each week. Well, she soon tired of so much moving about and quit. So we decided to do it differently this time. You will stay here with us until my friend's betrothed comes from New York, in about a month. Then you will live about four weeks with another family. Wait until you see how they treat you! Like a queen, I promise!" She laughed. "*I* should be so lucky!"

Kate sipped her hot tea. "I understand. It's just that though the agent didn't actually say it, he gave me the impression that I'd be living on my own at the schoolhouse." She couldn't for the life of her remember exactly what Mr. O'Brien had told her, but he had painted a pleasant picture, which she had framed in her memory throughout the long journey.

"That's because we want to build a meetinghouse that can also be used as a church and school. It's in the final planning stages."

"Where will I teach until it's built?"

Margo served Kate a large honey bun on a plate. "Would you believe that we still haven't decided?"

Kate looked up from her attack on the delicious, warm, sticky pastry. "After the experiences of this trip, I'd believe anything."

Margo continued. "We have three locations under consideration and decided to wait until you arrived before selecting. We thought you'd like to have some say in the matter."

"Thank you. That is very thoughtful. I *would* like to see them."

Margo folded her hands before her and smiled serenely. "Until then, how would you like to learn to run the store?"

Kate nearly choked on her tea. "Run the store?"

"Not alone, of course, we'd be here," she added with a

chuckle. "I thought it might be fun for you, and this being canning season as well as time to mend the boys' clothing for school. . . . I thought it would be both helpful for me and a time filler for you." She gazed at Kate apologetically. "I won't be able to entertain you at all."

Considering Margo's position as hostess and all the work she had to do, Kate understood. "Of course, I'd love to learn."

Margo smiled. "I'm so glad!" She stood. "Would you like more to eat?" When Kate shook her head, she continued, "I'll show you the room I've fixed for you. It isn't grand, but I hope you'll like it."

"You shouldn't have . . . ," Kate began earnestly.

"I loved every minute of it! I enjoy this sort of thing. And I didn't do it just for you—remember our friend's betrothed is coming soon." Margo led Kate from the kitchen through a large dining room, all spotlessly clean and well furnished. A small but cozy living room reached to the rear of the building, with a stairway spiraling down with polished wooden banisters.

"Your home is beautiful," Kate commented.

"Thank you. One's home is his world; is it not? He should feel comfortable and gain pleasure from it. Mr. Dutton, myself, and the boys enjoy ours. God has truly blessed us." Margo led Kate up the glossy wooden stairs.

Kate's heart lurched at the mention of God. Could she have been placed into a Christian home? Fearing disappointment, she didn't explore the matter.

Margo led her to a bedroom across the front portion of the house, which looked as if it might have been empty or used for storage before her arrival, as the carpet leading to it was hardly worn. The eaves sloped downward on both sides, giving a cozy look. A double bed with a wooden headboard stood to the far left, and a carved mahogany dresser with dangling metal drawer handles regally commanded the room's center. To the far right a wardrobe with a floor-length mirror graced one wall. Pink and white roses neatly papered the room, meeting the white wood trim and molding. The white bedspread's border of dangling yarn almost touched the highly polished hardwood floor, covered here and there with pink throw rugs.

Kate's throat tightened. "It's . . . lovely. I've never slept in such a delightful room."

"I'm so glad you like it. Makes every hour spent well worth it." Margo sighed with relief. "After dinner you must tell me all about yourself and your family. Will you?" She asked hesitantly.

"I'd love to," Kate replied, already liking Margo Dutton.

"Let's go back and mind the store while Mr. Dutton brings up your luggage," Margo announced, leading the way without waiting for an answer. Kate loved the way Margo took charge.

At the store customers came and went.

This is an excellent way to meet the people of Hays City, Kate decided.

As Margo waited on a customer, Kate's mind wandered. *My new room's the perfect place to curl up with a book.* She anticipated many hours of enjoyment. On the stagecoach, she'd finished *Jane Eyre* and begun *Wuthering Heights*, but the motion of the vehicle had often kept her from her favorite pastime.

She shivered with anticipation. Tucked away in her trunk were *Agnes Grey*, an assortment of dime novels, as well as her Bible and Shakespeare.

At home she'd often escaped from daily monotony by immersing herself in a good romance or adventure. In her mind she'd seen Ivanhoe win the fair Rowena, played the part of Juliet to a most handsome Romeo, and cried over countless near-lost loves. Once she left the Duttons', would her new hosts afford her the time and privacy for her books?

Just then a loud, jovial group of men thundered into the store, grabbing everyone's attention. Margo hugged each, while exchanging hearty greetings. Unlike the other customers all three were as fancily dressed as any Kate had seen in Chicago. They sported leather boots, colorful vests, ascots, starched white shirts, and the finest riding pants and jackets Kate had ever seen. Who were these handsome fellows with their aristocratic bearing?

Momentarily forgotten, Kate had time to study them carefully. The fair-haired man was tall with a square jaw and brown eyes. The shortest man had brownish hair and a thin, curling mustache. But the one who held her attention was of medium height, with hair so black it appeared blue when the sun hit it just right. Long, curled lashes, shaded large and water-blue eyes, by far his best feature. When he smiled, the slightest dimples creased each fleshy cheek. Kate fought not to stare at the handsomest man she'd ever seen.

Suddenly everyone seemed to notice her. Margo apologized and introduced her as the new schoolteacher, Miss Hunter. Kate's hostess pointed to the blond man. "This is Mr. Reginald Safford. Mr. Mitchell Hadden," Margo nodded toward the mustached man. "And my dear friend Geoffrey Grandville." Margo pinched his cheeks. "These fine gentlemen are from Victoria, which is about twelve miles from Hays. Originally they hail from England." Each man in turn took Kate's hand and, to her surprise, kissed the back of it. When Geoffrey's soft lips touched her hand,

Dangerous Illusions

goosebumps rippled up her arm and down to her toes. Kate fought to keep from blushing.

The glance that met hers, when she finally looked up, was warm and gentle. Kate felt as if his eyes had touched her soul. Had she known him for a lifetime—or only a few moments?

"You'll see plenty of me, for I am a frequent customer and caller." Geoffrey's hand still held hers, and his eyes sparkled.

Kate knew the thrill of feeling precious to a man. *Our hearts agree!* her mind exclaimed. *Why else would he have looked that way?*

Watching Geoffrey turn reluctantly to his friends, she thought of the heroes from her books. *None is as fine as he: handsome, charming, and wealthy. What more could a girl ask for? I've finally met the man of my dreams.*

Katherine Grandville, she tried the name on for size and thought it suited her.

Intent on her thoughts, Kate hardly noticed the turn of the conversation until one word drew her attention: *bride.* Mentally she replayed the conversation that had preceded it.

Margo had said, "When is your bride coming?"

Kate looked at the men. Who would answer? Which expected a bride? Finally one spoke, and Kate felt as if her newfound dream had turned into a nightmare.

2

"*L*ydia claims she'll be here in about a month—give or take a week," Geoffrey said. "Her father wants her to wait for the railroad to open, but—"

"Gracious, no!" cried Margo. "We have only a few months to plan for this wedding! She'll be coming in by stage, then?"

Geoffrey nodded. "But don't expect her in a month to the date. She's never been on time in her life! Yet she did promise me she'd be here by Thanksgiving at the latest."

Margo gasped. "But that's a month and a half late!"

"That's Lydia!" Geoffrey's cheeks dimpled as he smiled.

Kate remained flawlessly cheerful until she was alone that night in her bed. After crying softly for several moments, she sighed and punched her pillow, reasoning: *It isn't as if he's married already. Anything could happen. What if Lydia never arrives or changes her mind? If he loves me, things could be different.*

In the next few days Kate Hunter worked beside Margo in the store and began meeting many of her pupils.

Early the morning after her arrival a woman hustled into the store, dragging two well-dressed girls. "Are you the new teacher?" she asked boldly, tucking her straight blond hair behind her ears to hold it back from her face.

Kate smiled and nodded.

The woman pushed the children forward. "This here's Ellie and Martha. I'm their ma, Jane Kessler."

"Pleased to meet you." Kate shook each hand gingerly. "I'm looking forward to school, are you?" she asked the girls.

They nodded shyly.

"I'm twelve," the tallest one offered hesitantly. "I can read well." She pointed behind her. "Ma taught me."

"Excellent, you can help with the younger pupils." Kate knew she'd said the right thing when Ellie smiled broadly.

"Are you gonna live with us, too?" blurted the darker-haired, younger sister. When Kate shrugged and smiled, the girl continued, "We can't wait. Ma says you'll like our house better than the Groom's place, 'cause their house is like a hog's pen."

"Martha!" Jane Kessler's youthful-looking face turned crimson. "You mustn't say such things." Her faded blue eyes saddened as she apologized. "I'm sorry, Miss Hunter. Martha's nearly eight and ought to know better." Scratching her head, the mother claimed, "I just don't know what to do with her. She comes up with the most embarrassing things."

"I understand," Kate empathized. "Martha reminds me of my sister, Em. At fifteen, she still manages to speak her mind, no matter what."

"Of course," Jane continued rapidly, "the Groom's

house isn't like a hog's pen." She lowered her voice and leaned toward Kate. "It's just that Olive Groom doesn't—"

"Would the girls like to sample my new candy, Jane?" Margo interrupted. "I tried something new—a fruit-flavored glaze over caramel."

Ellie and Martha perked up and yanked at their mother's dress to make sure she'd heard Margo's offer.

Gazing at the eager faces, Jane agreed, and the girls jumped about excitedly.

Kate wondered what Jane Kessler would have told her about Olive Groom's housekeeping. Soon she'd be boarding with the Groom family. Was there something she should know? Was boarding around such a good idea?

Later that day a well-dressed elderly woman came into the shop. Margo greeted her with small talk, then introduced Kate to Hester O'Neill, wife of Paddy O'Neill of Paddy's Saloon and Gambling House. In a husky, no-nonsense voice, she ordered six loaves of bread, then scoured the shelves with her eyes.

"Something else today, Hester?" Margo prodded.

"Need a big cake. Bigger than any of these, and I have to have it by suppertime," she said gruffly. "Annie, one of my dancers, has a birthday today. We're going to surprise her."

"Hm-m-m." Margo scratched her head. "Usually they have to be ordered in advance. I *could* put two cakes together and frost them so they look like one. Would that do?" she asked.

"Sounds good to me. Can you put together one chocolate and one vanilla with chocolate icing?" Hester O'Neill asked, hands on hips.

"Sure. I'll take these into the kitchen and be back in a few minutes." Margo ducked into the kitchen, the cakes held high above her head.

"So you're the new teacher." The matronly looking woman's eyes scanned Kate from head to toe.

Kate nodded.

"Hope you like the job better than the last one did." Hester leaned forward, her gray eyes cold as steel. "Though I must admit, the families here are a strange sort—enough to scare anyone, I guess." She patted her tightly curled white hair. "Especially since the teacher has to board around. Hah! I knew that wouldn't work, but they're trying it again." She shrugged. "Why should I care? I don't have small children."

Kate's throat tightened as Mrs. O'Neill fed her fears. "What do you mean the families are strange? How strange?"

"Oh!" She laughed. "Take Black Nancy. You heard about her?" When Kate shook her head, she continued, "I thought not! They ought to have warned you. Buzz Balcomb married the daughter of one of his former slaves. We call her Black Nancy. Ever live with a slave?" she asked pointedly.

"N-no."

"Thought as much. Did they tell you about Olive Groom's housekeeping?" At Kate's quick nod, she raised her eyebrows. "So they did warn you some. I bet they didn't tell you George Plumb is a drunk. Have you ever lived with a drunk?"

Kate shook her head, eyes wide and frightened.

"I thought not," the woman beamed with confidence. "Then I'm sure no one told you about Josh Redfield, whose wife and her gentleman friend disappeared mysteriously. How can a woman board in a household without a chaperon?" Hester O'Neill leaned over the counter and practically whispered, " 'Sides, folks say he had something to do with—"

"Hester!" exclaimed Margo from the doorway, carefully balancing the large cake. "I told you before I won't allow gossip. Why, Kate's face is as pale as a sheet! What *have* you been telling her?"

"Now, Margo, I wasn't gossiping. It's fact that Mrs. Redfield—"

"No! Please!" Margo shook her head firmly. "Enough! Here's your cake and bread. I'll put them on your bill."

Shrugging, Hester O'Neill picked up her packages and left the shop.

"Kate, are you all right?" Margo sighed. "Don't listen to her or any of the other busybodies."

Kate dropped onto a nearby stool. "But how can I live in a hog's pen, with a Black Nancy, a drunk, or with a man whose wife disappeared mysteriously?"

Margo shook her head. "She told you all that in the few minutes it took me to frost the cakes?"

Kate nodded.

"Dear Lord, give me the strength, wisdom . . . ," she murmured, looking upwards. "Kate, it's unfair to judge people before meeting them, especially based on hearsay, rumors, or gossip."

"But what if the talk *is* true?"

"And what if it isn't? A judge always hears both sides of a case before deciding who's guilty and who's not. Not everything you hear is true. As gossip spreads from one person to another it often becomes distorted and exaggerated. Sometimes it's totally wrong, and when it isn't, it's God's business to judge, not ours."

Kate tilted her head. "How do you hear the other person's version?"

"If you feel it's your business, you ask him yourself."

"That isn't always possible," Kate countered. "Shall I ask Mrs. Groom if her home is truly a hog's pen?"

"Certainly not!"

"But," Kate argued, "if I'm to live in their home, it is my business. Right?"

Margo shook her head sadly. "Yes, I suppose—but it would hurt her to know someone had said such a thing. I suggest you use your time here with us to get to know these people and perhaps gain insight and learn the truth yourself." Margo patted the troubled girl's hand. "Don't worry, Kate, God will watch out for you. All you need to do is ask Him. And don't forget, their images may not be as smudged as people have painted them."

Margo continued, "Though many of the town people have affectionately labeled Mrs. Balcomb *Black Nancy*, I don't approve. She's from a different race and culture and has a different appearance. The godly here in Hays call her simply Nancy. I'd appreciate it if you'd do the same—at least while you stay with us."

Kate smiled. "So I've had my first prayer answered. I've landed in a Christian home."

Margo embraced Kate. "We have to stick together! Lord knows how few of us there are out here!"

That afternoon Margo invited Kate to ride with her on her deliveries, promising they'd visit the schoolhouse sites. The two women bumped along on the old buckboard's seat while the twins, in back, held down the precious cargo of baked goods. Their first stop landed them on the doorstep of Lucy's Restaurant. Kate remained in the wagon while Margo carried an armload of cakes and pies into the old, unpainted building. The steam on the inside of the front window kept Kate from seeing more than an elderly woman receiving the packages from behind two swinging doors at the rear of the restaurant. When they opened, she saw various men sat at checkered-cloth-covered tables, eating as though they hadn't seen food in days.

The next stop was Evans' Grocery Store and Post Office. Margo returned from her delivery with a handful of mail. "A letter from Lydia!" she cried, waving an envelope high above her head. "We'll save it for after devotions." She folded it inside her reticule, along with several coins.

The last stop was a small, ramshackle shanty at the edge of town, near the railroad station. Margo explained. "Harley Mullins broke his leg last month and hasn't been able to work at the lumberyard. His wife, Clara, is with child again, and they have four other small children. Whatever I have left over I give to an unfortunate family. I try to bring something to the Mullins as often as I can." Margo laughed and covered her mouth, whispering, "They also get our mistakes!"

"There can't be many of them," said Kate.

"Oh, enough! Like the day Luther Aldrich ordered a birthday cake for his daughter. His wife was too ill to make one—for she makes the best herself—and Elmer put the wrong daughter's name on the cake. Of course we quickly frosted a new one, but who wants a cake with Irma Aldrich's name on it? Clara Mullins claimed it was the best she'd ever tasted!

"Then I tease Harley that the hair on his chest comes from eating all the burned baked goods!"

After the Mullins stop, they pulled up in front of the lumberyard. Margo jumped down. "Here's schoolhouse number one."

Kate stepped down from the high seat. "A lumberyard?"

"Come." Margo led Kate swiftly to the rear of the yard.

The smell of freshly cut wood lingered in the air, although the place had apparently closed for the day.

Kate followed Margo, dodging between the boards and logs. Not as practiced as her leader, Kate was pulled abruptly to a stop by a rough board snagging her dress. Freeing herself, she ran swiftly in the direction Margo had gone. Kate couldn't afford to get lost amid the splintering timber. Yet she needn't have worried, for Margo's footprints in the sawdust were easily followed.

Several hundred feet behind the lumberyard, Kate saw their destination and shivered with apprehension. Lodged between two giant oak trees stood a small shanty. Kate hesitated, disappointment surging through her.

"Never judge a book by its cover, Kate," scolded Margo. "At least look inside."

Kate stepped into the shanty ahead of Margo, and as her foot rocked on loose planking she grabbed the doorjamb with a gasp. Margo steadied her. "Now, it may need work, Kate."

Glancing around inside, Kate decided that her first impression had been deceiving. The room wasn't as small as she'd thought, but it lacked the space needed by eighteen students. Bare, except for storage boxes, the shack was dark and musty.

"I don't have to decide before seeing the other two sites, do I?" Kate asked.

"No, of course not. Keep in mind the men will fix the school in time—if we select the one we want early enough, that is."

Margo led Kate back to the wagon, where the twins were sword fighting with tree branches.

They rode some distance before Margo reined in the team with expertise. "Now, Kate, keep an open mind."

Even when the dust cleared Kate saw nothing. Standing atop the wagon seat, she turned every which way.

"I don't see anything."

Margo laughed. "C'mon." Jumping down, she ran through the field, and Kate followed, with the twins close at her heels. They stopped at what looked like a grassy mound, and Kate noticed a door leading into the hill. Opening it, Margo invited her inside.

"What is this?" Kate peeked within.

"An abandoned dugout home."

"Whose was it?" Kate noted that while the room was still darker than she'd like, it was spacious and cool.

"A family named *Yeager* left it to go back East."

Hands on hips, Kate twirled about. "It's large enough, but awfully dark for a school. Children need proper light to work by."

"The men may be able to solve that problem." Margo shrugged. "We can mention it."

"What is this material covering the dirt floor?" Kate poked at the damp stuff with the toe of her boot.

"Burlap," Margo answered. "But perhaps the men could lay wood. You must keep in mind we haven't begun to remodel for school purposes yet."

Touching the cold dirt walls with her fingers, Kate shivered. She felt trapped in a dungeon and suddenly needed fresh air and sunlight. Heading for the doorway, she called over her shoulder, "I'll keep this all in mind. Can we get on to the next site?"

When Margo turned the team around toward town, Kate gave her a puzzled look.

"Yes, I deliberately passed by the third one to get to the dugout. The next site is closer to town than this one, but I wanted you to see it last."

"Why?" Kate asked.

"I guess for the sake of comparison. You'll no doubt like this one best, but it has its downfall, too."

"What is that?" she asked.

Margo smiled wryly. "It's owned by Joshua Redfield."

3

*B*ringing the rumbling buckboard to a halt, Margo pointed across the barren land. "See that house yonder, just above the horizon?"

Kate nodded.

"That's the new Redfield home. Now follow the horizon to the left. See the old homestead? That's the third school site. Better than a dugout, it's built with sod bricks and much like the houses back East, with windows and a thatched roof." Picking up the reins, Margo added, "Wait until you see it."

As they rolled down the long road leading to the homes, Kate inquired, "How far are we from town?"

"Only a mile and a quarter. See there? You can see the buildings from here, the land is so flat."

"Which of the three sites is most centrally located?"

To be heard above the noise of the horses, buckboard, and the twins, Margo shouted, "I'd say the dugout is probably the closest for most, but the Redfields' is a close second. The lumberyard would be convenient only for the few children who live in town. I'm glad you're thinking of considerations other than appearance."

They stopped before a house Kate thought could have come from a Dickens novel. It looked like an English peasant's farmhouse, with its thatched roof and neatly placed "bricks."

Facing the front stood a doorway with a large window on each side, with four panes on the top and four on the bottom. As she entered, Kate saw a fairly large room that glowed with sunlight.

"This still isn't big enough for all my students." Kate spoke regretfully, for other than that, it seemed the best of the three.

"I mentioned that to Josh," Margo responded, putting one hand on the back wall. "He said there'd be no problem taking out these partitions. They really don't do much at all to support the house."

As they passed on into the other small rooms Kate noted that the tall side windows and rear windows would provide a large, one-room building with plenty of light. Kate could only wonder why she hadn't been shown this spotlessly clean house first. Why was there any question at all as to which building should be the schoolhouse?

Margo beamed proudly. "Joanna Redfield worked months on this woven rag rug, and it covers nearly all of the wood-planked floor. The walls are adobe plaster and solid. Look, the windows open, too!"

Kate tapped her foot impatiently. "Why didn't we come here first? You knew what my reaction would be to the other two. What's the trick?"

Margo excused herself to scold the boys, who played too

roughly in the wagon, then returned and faced the school-teacher. "I wanted you to fully appreciate it."

"You didn't think I'd have the sense to select this one, even if I'd seen it first or second?" Kate exclaimed in disbelief.

"Possibly. Yet there are those in the district who aren't in favor of accepting Josh Redfield's generous gift. We had many heated meetings over this. Finally the board members agreed to let you decide."

"I've decided. This is it."

"The fact that it belongs to Josh Redfield doesn't matter to you?"

"Will he be a bother?" she asked with concern.

"Certainly not!" Margo said vigorously.

"Then why should it matter?"

"Because of the talk. Remember Mrs. O'Neill's remarks?"

Kate nodded. "As long as he doesn't interfere with the school, I don't care!"

"She isn't the only one accusing Josh Redfield of having something to do with his wife's disappearance. Some parents may protest."

"Do *you* believe it's true?" Kate probed.

"No, I don't. I'm merely judging the man by what he is and always has been: a gentleman. The circumstances *do* seem bizarre, but my faith is in my first and only impression of Josh. Even if I were wrong, and the talk proved true, I'm still not his judge. I'll let God be his judge and jury. There isn't much conventional law out here, so we have little choice but to let God take over entirely; and let me tell you, the punishment in eternity will be worse than any here!"

Kate shivered. "Do you think Mrs. Redfield is dead or has simply run off?"

"It's difficult for me to believe any of the gossip. Joanna is such a lovely young woman. You would take to her, Kate. Yet who knows anyone's personal affairs or hardships? Whether Joanna is alive or dead, though, I don't think Josh Redfield could physically harm anyone."

"What are the Redfield children like?"

"There's just Anna. A lovely five-year-old girl, who has taken the tragedy badly. She hardly speaks to anyone, except Josh, whom she adores." With a sigh Margo added, "I think she'll turn out fine. You should see the way she fusses over her dad. . . ."

Margo shook her head sadly. "I won't say any more; I'll let you form your own opinions. Just promise me one thing?"

Kate nodded.

"Don't listen to any more gossip."

The thought that someone so close could be a murderer frightened Kate, and she yearned to know the truth. Yet she agreed with Margo: The man deserved a fair chance. Gossip would, indeed, color her opinion of Josh Redfield. *Had* it been unfair of Mrs. O'Neill to "warn" her?

That evening Kate's heart pounded as she arrived in the dining room for dinner. There stood Geoffrey Grandville, bending over Margo's hand. Kate froze with delight in the doorway.

"Geoffrey, I'm so glad you could join us tonight," cried Margo, beaming. "I received a letter from Lydia today!"

"That makes two of us." He grinned widely. "What did yours say?"

"I haven't read it yet. I thought we'd share it after dinner and devotions."

"That should be interesting, but you will make the devotions short tonight, won't you? I've had a rough day and have to tuck in early tonight, for tomorrow is another big day." He turned.

"Nice to see you again, Kate. What a truly delightful dress—on a delightful lady, I might add. Why, I do believe even the ladies of London could not surpass you."

Kate basked in his words.

"Do sit beside me. I'm so lonely for female company." When Geoffrey saw Margo's frown and her hands on her hips, he added, "Single females, that is!"

Margo cuffed him lightly. "Another woman enters the room and already you forget me!"

"Never, Margo. You shall always remain my favorite love, but naturally Elmer is reluctant to part with you."

"Good shop help is hard to find." Elmer laughed as he entered from the living room. "Good to see you, Geoff. Good hunting today?"

"Two rabbits and a prairie chicken." He beamed. "Tomorrow we'll take a gun." Everyone laughed, and Kate joined them when she realized Geoffrey had been joking.

During dinner Geoffrey remained attentive, and Kate found it hard not to seem too preoccupied with this man who drew her like a magnet.

"Tell me about your family. Are you from the West?" he asked, sincere interest lighting his sparkling blue eyes.

Kate shook her brown head, causing the curls to bounce slightly. "No. I'm from the Chicago area. My family has a farm a few miles from the city."

"A farmer!" Geoffrey exclaimed. "How quaint! What type of farm?"

"Mainly dairy, but we harvest a lot of wheat and corn, too. My folks are hard working and successful. They sent me to school to receive my teaching certificate, and they plan to send my sister, Em, too."

"Sister Em? Kate and Em?" Geoffrey laughed. "Are those your real names?"

Kate smiled. "My name is Katherine, and my sister is Emily. We were both named for grandmothers. *Emily* is Dad's mother, and *Katherine* is my maternal grandmother."

"How American!" Geoffrey teased. "And what are your parents' names . . . ? Oh, do let me guess!" He put his index finger to his temple. "*Clementine* and *Andrew*, and you call them Clem and Andy!"

Kate giggled. "No, silly. I'm not telling you their names, for you'll mock them!"

Helping himself to more meat and potatoes, Geoffrey mildly scolded, "I'm not making fun! Merely trying to lighten the tension of new friendship. I am truly interested in you Americans and your ways. I'm intrigued with this country so far. *Do* tell me the names of your family."

"Mom's name is *Lovinia*," she tested. When he didn't laugh, she continued. "My father is *Benjamin Hunter*."

"No nicknames for them?" His eyes were compelling.

She smiled, admitting, "Yes, *Lovey* and *Ben*, and my little brother is *Benji*."

"And Benji will inherit the farm?" he asked, buttering his bread casually.

Kate nodded.

"That's the way it is in England, too. Which is why I came here. My oldest brother inherits my father's whole estate, and they've married off my other brother—quite well, I might add. When it came to me, I had two choices. The military or the ministry." Geoffrey politely touched his napkin to his lips. "No offense intended, but I don't feel any enthusiasm for either." Geoffrey's mouth quirked with humor. "They are both honorable professions, but not for Geoffrey Grandville!"

"So you came here?" She tilted her head to study him.

"A land agent came to England and sold me and my two friends on Kansas. We arrived with a rather large group and love this country. We hunt and have started a polo club and a tennis club. Now we're building a hall to hold dances and parties. The first big event will be my wedding, of course."

Astonished, Kate dropped her fork and stared at him. "But how are you living? I was under the impression being a settler was hard work. Most of the ones I've met so far haven't time for polo, tennis, and parties."

His brow creased into an affronted frown. "Of course we work. We spend at least three or four hours a day sowing, hoeing, planting, and all that. It is, indeed, hard work." His face brightened. "Yet because we all work together, it needn't consume our whole day. We have fox hunts. Of course instead of fox, we hunt rabbit, squirrel, or whatever else happens to run when we chase it. We make time for fun and sports. Can you imagine an Englishman who lost his love of sport? Why, it's just not to be thought of! Buying our baked goods from Margo saves our women time, so they can keep themselves looking ravishing." Geoffrey's eyes flashed with humor. "Yet I don't know why there aren't any single gentleman to court them!"

"There's yourself and your two friends." Kate's eyes told him everything she felt.

For an instant, Geoffrey's gaze sharpened. "Well, I'll soon be wed, and my friends claim to be confirmed bachelors. Yet I wonder about Safford. He's been sprucing up too frequently and visiting the home of a Miss India Biggs. I'm thinking he isn't long for bachelorhood either."

"And there are no other unmarried men in Victoria?" she

asked, wondering how she compared with his betrothed.

Geoffrey put his finger to his face. "We had another, but he disappeared. . . . No, Kate, no others. Such a shame, for some of the lassies are quite comely."

"One disappeared?" Kate asked.

"Yes, I'm sure you've heard the talk. No one in Hays City could miss it entirely. About six months ago Phillip Barringer vanished without a trace, leaving his home and livestock behind. Some speculate he ran off with a married woman; others say the husband put a permanent end to them both."

Recalling what she'd heard about the Redfields, Kate wanted to question him further, but a warning look from Margo silenced her.

"Geoffrey, you know how I feel about gossip," Margo said with warning in her voice. "It isn't fair to discuss someone who isn't here to defend himself."

"You are absolutely correct, Mrs. Dutton, and I apologize most humbly," Geoffrey Grandville mocked as he stood and bowed in Margo's direction. "I forgot myself. Will you forgive me?"

Kate marveled at his charm and found a joyous satisfaction in his quick wit and humor.

"Most certainly," answered Margo with eyes a-twinkle. "Do be seated so we can serve dessert."

Throughout the evening Geoffrey remained at Kate's side, dazzling her with his repartee.

Does he act this way with his betrothed? Kate wondered. She'd never known a man to be this attentive to a mere friend. Could Geoffrey lack admiration for her and still want to know all about her life?

Her mind went back to home. Vaguely she remembered a story about some neighbors, a couple nearly her parents' age. According to Kate's mother, everyone in town had known how the quiet Helen had pined for Edward Taggart. Yet he'd fallen in love with the beautiful Cassandra. When that fickle beauty had run off with another man, just before the wedding day, Edward had turned to Helen again. *Why today they're the happiest couple for miles around*, Kate thought. *Couldn't things turn out that way for me, too? All I need to do is be as steadfast as Helen was.* When Geoffrey needed her, she'd be there.

After Geoffrey had left, Margo spoke of him. Despite her usual distaste for describing the affairs of others, she praised the man and the positive influence he had in Victoria. "We're so glad he was one of the settlers," she added. "His father is an earl, you know, and I'm certain he could have had a fine career in England—though he'd never boast of such a thing. Why, even if he didn't want the military or the ministry, he could have stood for election to the House of Commons. He'd make a fine leader.

"The ladies of London must have felt the loss of him. Every woman in Victoria and Hays City is half in love with his way of making them feel special. But it's all just a knack he learned in his father's house. I've never seen anyone more faithful to a woman than he is to Lydia."

Margo's words became almost pointed. "A woman would have to be foolish to think he meant anything else. Geoffrey's faithfulness is one of his most appealing qualities."

She went on to talk about other matters, but Kate was hardly listening. *How does Margo know?* she wondered. *After all, she's never even met Lydia.*

* * *

The next afternoon Kate worked in the store while Margo and Elmer baked and decorated cakes. A tall, burly man with reddish-brown hair came in and sauntered over to the counter.

His quiet voice had an ominous quality. "Is Mrs. Dutton in?"

Kate's smile froze as she looked up into a face that reminded her of a bear. A thick blond beard and mustache made the man appear brutish and insensitive, and Kate shivered with fear. Only when her eyes met his did she find any warmth. Large brown eyes sparkled below the bushy eyebrows and offered a tinge of friendliness.

Controlling her emotions, Kate replied coolly, "Yes, she's in the kitchen. May I tell her who's calling?"

The thick, bushy eyebrows furrowed deeply. "Joshua Redfield."

"One moment." Kate scampered off towards the kitchen door. "Margo," she called. "You have a caller. A J-Josh Redfield," she managed to say.

Margo flew out to meet her visitor. "Josh, how are you?" She shook his hand firmly.

"Fine. Good to see you again," he uttered without hesitation. Kate could tell by his tone that he liked Margo.

They made small talk until Redfield punched his hat with his hand nervously. "Has a decision been made on the school site?"

"Yes, it's settled. We will gratefully accept your generous offer of your old home for our schoolhouse, and I'd like you to meet the deciding vote." Margo turned and held out her hand. "Josh Redfield, our new schoolteacher, Kate Hunter." As Kate accepted Josh's firm handshake, Margo continued, "I took Kate out to the old homestead, and she loved it. Didn't you, dear?"

Kate merely nodded, intimidated by his powerful presence.

Joshua's eyes gleamed with pleasure. "Is there anything I can do to make it more suitable for a school?"

"Just this morning we made a list of changes and repairs. I'll run into the kitchen and get it, if you'll excuse me for one second." Margo disappeared through the door, leaving Kate uncomfortably alone with the giant, lumbering, mountainlike man.

To Kate's relief, another customer entered the store. She recognized Hester O'Neill and prepared to greet her cheerfully. But Hester and Josh Redfield's eyes met, and both glared. Turning their backs to each other, they browsed among the baked goods.

Confronted by such animosity, Kate welcomed the sight of her hostess returning with the list. Margo handed the paper to Joshua. "School should open a week from Monday. Will that give you enough time?"

Joshua's eyebrows gathered again as his eyes scanned the list. "I think school will open on time. Most of these changes are minimal." Joshua folded the paper, put it in his breast pocket, and bowed. "Nice meeting you, Miss Hunter." He nodded toward Margo. "Feel free to come out any time, for any reason. The building is now the school district's, for the purpose of teaching the children of Hays."

When the door closed behind him, Margo returned to the kitchen, and a low cough reminded Kate that Hester O'Neill was still in the store. She bustled forward. "I'll have five loaves of bread, please."

Kate packaged the bread swiftly. "That will be twenty-five cents."

Mrs. O'Neill handed her the coins and took her packages.

Before turning away, she asked, "So you've decided to use the old Redfield house for the school."

"Yes, ma'am, it's by far the best choice," Kate conceded.

"You're sure of that, are you?" Hester's eyes pierced Kate's. "Teaching young children on a murderer's property is the best choice?"

Kate's heart pounded and she felt perspiration forming on her upper lip. "But we don't know that for fact. . . . Margo says—"

"I know what Margo thinks, but I have all the proof *I* need. The man is a murderer. He found his wife with her lover and killed them both rather than lose her."

Kate looked about uncomfortably. "How can you say such a thing?"

"Both Mrs. Redfield and Mr. Barringer left without a trace, leaving behind certain possessions. Joanna Redfield would never leave without her daughter or her wedding ring."

"Her wedding ring?" Kate asked, green eyes wide.

"You haven't heard?" She leaned closer. "Mrs. Redfield's wedding ring was found in Joshua's pocket when the sheriff searched him the next day. How do you suppose it got from her finger into his pocket?"

As she opened the door, Hester O'Neill's gray eyes squinted coldly, *"Best choice,* indeed." She disappeared, and Kate felt her heart pound with anxiety.

Talking to Margo, she'd felt right about Redfield. Now, after hearing Hester, Kate felt unsure. Had she made an error? Was the lofty, fierce-looking man a murderer? She shivered.

4

Kate gazed at the prairie around her as Margo drove the wagon down the long road toward the new schoolhouse. At least she would have no surprise visitors; the land was so barren and flat an approaching rider could be seen for miles. Her gaze wandered from the schoolhouse to the Redfield's new home. The stately two-story homestead loomed before her, beckoning invitingly, about an eighth of a mile from the school, separated from it by only a field and a barn. The pillars shone with new paint and shutters hung at every window. *Such an enormous dwelling,* Kate thought, *for a man and a small girl. It looks as though Josh Redfield had planned for a large family.* Had Mr. Barringer foiled those plans? She scolded herself and realized Margo had stopped the wagon before the freshly painted door of the new schoolhouse.

"Look!" Margo exclaimed excitedly. "Someone has hung a chime!"

A large metal plate hung beside the front door, with a wooden mallet hanging from a rope nearby.

"Let's try it!" Kate cried.

"*You* have to do it. You're the teacher," quipped Margo.

Kate grabbed the mallet and hit the metal plate firmly. The chime rang loud and clear. "I love it!" exclaimed Kate, her eyes clear and bright.

Margo stepped quickly inside, and Kate followed, reluctant to take her eyes from the shiny chime.

Both ladies marveled at the interior, now one large room. Fresh lumber scented the air. Individual wooden chairs were neatly placed in rows, behind newly constructed tables. At the front stood a large desk, for Kate, complete with drawers and bookends. Upon the desk sat a green vase with a single red rose tucked inside. At the edge of the desk sat a wooden plaque. Kate picked it up and turned it over. "Oh, look, Margo!" she cried. "It has my name on it: MISS HUNTER."

"How thoughtful!" Margo looked about. "Everything is simply perfect. Our list is completed—and then some!"

Kate rubbed her fingers along the smooth finish of her desk. "Who made this wonderful furniture?"

"Josh owns the lumberyard, and I suppose he had one of his men do the carpentry work."

"Why is this Josh Redfield so helpful where the school is concerned?" Kate wondered aloud.

"He's always been one of the biggest supporters of education in this area. He and Joanna have worked hard to bring a teacher to Hays, not only for the benefit of their daughter, Anna, but because they are both highly refined and educated people and realize the importance of a good education."

Kate nodded. "Very sensible." Gazing about, she

touched the draperies: Burlap. "Does Mr. Redfield sew, too?"

"No." Margo laughed. "But Ella Thompson, our church pianist, does."

"What's in the box?" Kate peered into a wooden carton beneath the back window. "Why, he's even supplied us with books. *McGuffy's Reader!* How wonderful! And a book of maps! How ever did he come by these splendid books?" she asked. "Oh, Margo!" she exclaimed, "He's even given us a Bible."

"At Sunday meeting we've been requesting donations for the school, yet I have a feeling these belong to Josh himself."

Kate opened the covers of the books. "Most have his name inside, but the Bible has *Joanna Redfield* written plainly in black ink."

Margo swung around and grabbed the book from Kate. "Joanna left without her favorite Bible?"

An approaching wagon broke the silence and the impact of Margo's discovery. She gazed out the window. "Looks as if we have company."

"Perhaps it's Josh Redfield?" Kate joined Margo at the window.

Margo shook her head. "He'd come the back way. I think it's Geoffrey. But why would he be driving a wagon?"

Kate's throat became dry. "Really?" She squinted. "So it is Geoffrey, and he's toting something in the wagon."

The ladies ran outside.

"Welcome to our new schoolhouse," Margo called.

As he reined in the panting horses, Geoffrey Grandville's mouth widened with pleasure. "I've brought over my contribution to education." He pointed to the large object lying on the bed of the buckboard.

The women stared for several moments before speaking. "A real chalkboard!" exclaimed Kate, finally. "I've never used one before!" In her excitement she threw her arms around Geoffrey's neck. "Oh, thank you! That's the most wonderful surprise yet!"

Geoffrey momentarily returned her embrace. "Certainly glad I went to the trouble! Never thought I'd be rewarded so generously." His eyes met hers warmly.

Kate quickly withdrew her hold on him. "Oh! I'm sorry! I didn't mean to be so forward, but I'm so thrilled. So few teachers have a real chalkboard! I must be dreaming!" She gasped, holding her heart to calm its pounding. Was the throbbing due to the excitement of the gift or her embrace with Geoffrey?

Margo spoke, reminding Kate of her presence. "Geoffrey, how wonderful. I didn't think you supported the school. You never came to the meetings. . . ."

"But Margo, my time is so precious. While I don't have myself to contribute, I *am* blessed with finances." The warmth of his smile echoed in his voice. "It was the least I could do."

"We certainly appreciate it," murmured Margo, as if genuinely surprised by Geoffrey's gesture.

"I, too, thank you, Mr. Grandville," a gruff voice agreed heartily from behind Kate. "Very thoughtful of you! In fact surprisingly so," Josh Redfield added almost sourly, approaching the wagon slowly.

How long had he been standing there? Kate wondered.

"Let me help carry it into the schoolhouse," Josh offered. When he grabbed one end of the large slate, his brown eyes met Kate's green ones. "If you show us where you want it, we'll attach it to the wall for you."

Slightly frightened by Josh's boldness, Kate flew ahead of

the men, and when she'd chosen a spot on the wall for the board, she merely pointed.

As the men set down the chalkboard Geoffrey held up one hand. "Sorry, good people, I'd love to assist in placing the thing, but I have a pressing engagement. . . . You will all excuse me, I hope?" He bowed politely.

"Certainly," said Margo. "Thank you again."

Kate held out her hands. Geoffrey took them, and her eyes blurred with tears. "You'll never know how thrilled I am by your generous, thoughtful gift. I never dreamed. . . ." Her voice broke, and she pulled out her handkerchief.

"My dear lady," replied Geoffrey gallantly, "had I known, I would have purchased a half dozen." He bowed again. "Farewell."

Kate patted her eyes as Geoffrey turned his wagon around and rolled down the long drive to the main road. "Such a dear, sweet man he is!" she murmured.

Josh nearly dropped the chalkboard. Kate saw him frown, then caught Margo throwing him a look of warning. He shook his head, grimaced, and continued with his work.

Kate sensed Josh Redfield's deep dislike for Geoffrey Grandville. She stiffened her back and busied herself with unpacking books. Why should a man with Josh's reputation like a fine man like Geoffrey? Josh was merely jealous of the Englishman, decided Kate.

When Kate arrived at the schoolhouse on Monday, children played in the fields nearby. Margo stopped the wagon by the door, and Kate, Carl, and Earl jumped down. Waving, Margo turned the wagon around and headed back to town and her bakery.

Kate counted heads as she walked toward the door: fifteen. *Not bad for the first day,* she thought. After arranging papers on her new desk, she straightened, took a deep breath, smoothed the front of her yellow gingham dress, then walked with assurance to the chime outside the door.

By the fifth ring she had everyone's attention, and they stood frozen, watching her from their places in the schoolyard. She smiled and motioned for them to enter the schoolhouse.

One by one they filed in. The older boys ducked their heads shyly and shuffled lazily, while the girls giggled and smiled for their young teacher. The smaller children stared and ran past swiftly, lest she notice something wrong with them.

Kate noted that while most of the children's clothing was by no means new or fine, each was clean and tidy—or at least she could tell they had been sent that way. A few boys showed signs of their rough play before school. Only a couple of the pupils dressed poorly or were in need of a good scrubbing.

When the last child had disappeared through the door, Kate entered. At the sight of the school's fine furnishings the pupils stood in awe.

"If everyone will line up against this wall, I'll call the roll and begin seating," Kate announced somewhat meekly.

As the pupils obeyed Kate spoke with new-gained confidence: "My name is *Miss Hunter.* When I touch your shoulder, I'd like you to introduce yourself and tell me your age."

Kate lightly touched the shoulder of the first boy.

"Peter Balcomb," he said shyly. "I'm eleven, but I'll be twelve on Saturday!" he exclaimed excitedly.

Kate pointed. "Peter, this is where I'd like you to sit."

Walking back to the line, she touched the shoulder of a somewhat raggedly dressed girl.

"Effie Groom, and I'm already twelve," she said politely.

"Thank you, Effie. You may take a seat next to Peter."

One by one the children gave their names and ages, and Kate noticed something special about each one.

Olive-skinned Peter Balcomb had big, expressive brown eyes and curly hair. Effie had manners, even if she lacked presentable clothes. Helen Aldrich was an eight-year-old who stuttered, and her older sister Irma had flaming red hair, brighter even than Carl and Earl's. While little Josie Aldrich hid behind ten-year-old Irma's skirt and wouldn't tell her name or age, Helen came forward and helped her little sister, leading her to the appointed seat.

Kate placed Ella Kessler with the others in her age group and noticed her deeply dimpled cheeks as she smiled at Peter Balcomb. Martha Kessler wore a dress of the exact same material as her sister Ella's; only the styles were different. Kate thought Jane Kessler had put a whole bolt of cloth to excellent use.

Willie, Lucy, and Jonathan Balcomb were respectively ten, seven, and five. Kate noticed their mother's African heritage in their "coffee with cream" complexions, dark eyes, and hair. Nancy had each dressed well, and their noses shone with cleanliness.

The Dutton twins, as Carl and Earl were called, were their usual shy, giggly selves. They seemed quite chummy with Georgie Plumb, an only child who was also ten years old. She seated them together, glad that by now she knew them well enough that their individual mannerisms identified them.

Mary Jane Haun, also ten, sat beside Georgie Plumb and had pigtails that almost reached the floor. Rollie Groom, clothes as disheveled as his sister Effie's, exuded courtesy and manners.

Kate stood back and admired them. An unusual bunch, to be sure, but she loved them all and could see good qualities in each. None seemed to be difficult, and she felt confident she could teach them and help them become better citizens of this grand nation, the United States of America.

Kate folded her hands. "Each morning, before we begin learning, we will bow our heads and thank God for our blessings and ask His help and guidance. For now, I'll say the prayer, but you must repeat it in your own heads and thus let God know I speak for you. Later, when we're better acquainted, we'll take turns saying the morning blessing."

As the children bowed their heads a disturbance at the main door drew all eyes. In walked Josh Redfield with a small girl in tow. Kate couldn't help but feel aggravated.

"Mr. Redfield, school begins at nine o'clock sharp," she chastised him firmly.

The children stared at him.

Color shaded Josh Redfield's face like a shadow, and for the first time Kate witnessed his lack of confidence. "I'm sorry—I, that is w-we—, ah-h," he faltered uncomfortably. Pushing the small girl forward gently, he cleared his throat. "This is Anna. Her mother taught her some, so she isn't starting from scratch—I mean—" he stuttered, at a complete loss for words. "S-she's five."

Kate could hardly believe this was the same man who seemed so terrifying just a few days ago.

Kate smiled warmly at Anna. "Thank you for coming, Anna. But do see if you can get your father ready on time, from now on."

The other children giggled, and Anna's frightened face

loosened somewhat, but still she didn't smile. Her large blue eyes were watery, as if she were about to break into tears at any moment.

"So Anna is five," Kate remarked to herself aloud. "Her mother has already taught her the essentials, so I shall try her with the middle age group. Anna, please take a seat here," she pointed, "beside Helen Aldrich and Martha Kessler."

Instead of moving toward the seat, Anna bolted straight for her father and the door. Kate called quickly after her, "Anna! Would you be in charge of the chalkboard this week?"

The child froze in her flight toward Josh Redfield. Slowly turning, she gave Kate a startled look. "Ch-chalkboard?" she asked.

"Why, yes. I'll need someone to wash it every day after school and care for the eraser rags. Everyone will get a chance, but I'd like you to be first." Kate smiled warmly. "Somehow I have the impression you've experience with a chalkboard and should show the others."

Anna's eyes brightened. "Oh, yes! I have a small slate at home."

"I thought so," said Kate. "Will you sit with the eight-year-old girls?"

Anna nodded and jumped into the chair beside Helen and Martha without giving Josh Redfield another glance.

Kate nodded sternly at Josh. With a look of approval, he tipped his hat and disappeared out the door.

5

*E*ven the children who lived several miles away walked to school. Despite the long trek ahead of them, Kate discovered they still looked forward to school. Some even expressed dismay as the weekend drew near. On bad-weather days many parents drove their children to or from school on a buckboard. On Friday it rained, and Kate had the opportunity to meet several more parents.

Archie Kessler arrived shortly before nine, with two girls beneath his large raincoat. "Been praying for rain, Miss Hunter?" He laughed, shaking the rain from his coat. "Your prayers have been answered! I'm Archie Kessler and glad to finally meet you. The girls talk so much about you, I had to come and see for myself if any of it were true." He shook her hand.

Shy Ella and Martha Kessler surely took after their mother, thought Kate. Yet she liked Archie Kessler and his outgoing ways. He reminded her of her brother, Benji.

Josh Redfield walked Anna to school every morning and

47

picked her up every afternoon. Kate thought perhaps it was because she was only five. In bad weather Josh drove a lovely carriage.

It continued to rain all day Friday, and Archie Kessler picked up his girls at three o'clock. Josh came by for Anna, and just as Kate was bundling up the Balcomb children against the rain, Nancy bustled in with her husband, Buzz Balcomb.

Kate had seen very few Negroes. She tried hard not to stare or look shocked. Nancy was tall, lithe, and extremely pretty. Buzz had dirty blond hair, and despite his acne-scarred complexion, Kate thought him boyishly handsome.

"I'm Nancy Balcomb; this is my husband, Buzz. We're happy to meet you, Miss Hunter. The children talk of nothing else but you these days."

Kate shook her hand. "Happy to meet you. It's reassuring to hear that my pupils don't forget me as soon as they leave here at three!"

Buzz extended his hand. "The amazing thing about it is they can't wait to come to school. You must be doing something right! I've never seen them so enthusiastic. I salute you for whatever it is that you do."

"Peter is one of the most helpful boys," said Kate. "Willie is a great reader, and Jonathan is a math whiz. Of course Lucy is our class artist."

"God bless you, Miss Hunter," Nancy said softly. "I can hardly wait until we have a turn having you in our home."

"To say nothing of the kids' excitement!" Buzz laughed.

After the Balcombs had left, Kate chastised herself. How could she have ever let gossip frighten her? Nancy was a lovely woman and Buzz an extraordinary man. She no longer feared staying with the family. *Margo is right again,* she thought.

As Kate packed the papers she'd need to correct into a cloth bag, she mentally reviewed her first week. All her fears had been needless. Not one parent had objected to her choice for the schoolhouse. Every child, with the exception of Georgie Plumb, was quite cooperative. Georgie, she'd learned, sassed back and balked whenever she gave him a chore, but eventually gave in.

Beautiful Anna could hardly be called a behavior problem, though she spoke hardly at all and often stared out of the window instead of doing her work. The only activity the child showed excitement about was taking care of the chalkboard. What would happen when Kate had to select a new helper, next week? It was only fair. But the schoolteacher knew somehow she'd need to reach Anna soon. Was the little girl missing her mother? Kate yearned to know the details, so she could help this bright child.

I'll ask Mr. Redfield to pick her up at four, on Monday, Kate decided. *That way I can talk with Anna.* Surely any teacher worth her salt could handle such a gentle, sensitive child.

Church services were now also held at the schoolhouse. Because there was no traveling preacher nearby this week, Ottmar Holman conducted the service. Kate noticed most of her pupils attended, with their parents, giving her an opportunity to study each family.

The Grooms did not attend, nor did the Plumb family. *How will I attend services when I'm staying with these families?* Kate wondered.

Carlton and Clara Haun sat in the front row, with Mary Jane. As Buzz and Nancy Balcomb slid into a place in the rear, with Peter, Jonathan, Willie and Lucy, they all waved at Kate. Archie and Jane Kessler took a place in front of Kate and the Duttons, and Kate marveled again at Jane's sewing ability when she saw the lovely dresses the girls wore. Luther and Berta Aldrich sat behind her, with Helen, Irma, and Josie. Though Josie kept poking her finger into Kate's shoulder, when Kate turned around, she'd hide her face and smile coyly. Kate noted how Josie slowly crept from her shell of shyness.

Almost unseen in the rear of the church, Josh Redfield and Anna sat with an elderly worman whom Kate didn't recognize.

As she sang some of her favorite hymns, nostalgia swept over Kate. After Ottmar's inspiring sermon, the congregation spoke their prayers faithfully and sincerely. Pleased with the time she'd spent in the meeting, Kate could hardly wait to return next week.

Riding back home after the service, Kate asked Margo about the woman with Josh and Anna.

"That's Ayda Simcox, Clara Mullins's mother. Remember the day we made deliveries and stopped to give their family our extras and mistakes? Ayda's a hard-working woman and good as they come. Despite all the gossip about the Redfields, she not only stays with them, but doesn't utter a word about the situation. She simply mumbles: 'Folks should clean their own houses before they try to sweep someone else's.' She's also a godly woman."

Monday morning, when Josh brought Anna—on time, to be sure—Kate asked for a word with him. When she motioned him to a far corner, he followed.

"Mr. Redfield, would it be possible for you to pick Anna up at four today, instead of three?"

"I suppose. Why?" he asked, his shaggy eyebrows creased into a frown.

"I need some time with her alone. She is unresponsive in class, and I need to get to know her better."

"Sure. I'll be here at four," he said, touching his forehead slightly in a mock salute and marching out the door.

When school was dismissed at three and the others had all left, Kate approached Anna and sat beside her. "Why don't you speak out in class like the others?" Kate asked gently.

Anna shrugged.

"You seem anxious to learn, yet you won't talk, but simply stare out the window in a daze. Is there a reason? Please tell me; I'm concerned about you."

Again Anna shrugged.

"Is it because you miss your mother?" Kate dared.

Anna's head swung toward Kate in surprise, and she nodded, eyes tear filled.

Sympathy swelled within Kate, and she regretted the need to bring up the subject. "I'm sorry, too, Anna. But if your mother were here, you know she'd want you to learn. Wouldn't she?" Kate prodded.

Anna nodded. "Mama taught me to read. I can even write!"

"So when she comes back . . . ," Kate began.

"Will Mama come back?" Anna looked hopeful.

"If you were my little girl, I'd surely return, if I could. Maybe she cannot."

She looked at Kate brightly. "Josh says she will."

"Josh? Don't you call him 'Father'?"

"Oh, no. He's Josh. But he's my father. Right?" she asked with wide, blue eyes.

"Yes, of course. My grandmother hated to be called 'Gram,' so she asked us to call her 'Nana.' It didn't make her any less our grandmother. It just pleased her more."

Anna smiled.

"Do you think I'm a good teacher, Anna?" Kate asked.

The small girl's blond curls bounced when she nodded vigorously.

"Then why don't you like anything but the chalkboard? If I'm a good teacher, you should want to learn."

Anna's eyes brimmed with unshed tears. "No! It isn't you!" The girl flung her arms around Kate's neck. "You're the best teacher in the world." She hesitated. "Except for my mother," she added in a whisper.

Kate returned Anna's embrace. "I know that you are a troubled young lady. I understand." Could she help Anna? Kate patted the small back and broke the embrace to search the girl's face. "Do you believe in God, Anna?" Kate asked, thinking of the only Comforter she knew.

Anna nodded. "Mama told me all about Him and His Son, Jesus." She smiled, despite her tear-filled blue eyes. "I love Jesus. He came in my heart, so I can go to heaven. He helps me be good."

"Did your mother also tell you that you can ask Him to help you when things hurt?"

Anna tilted her head. "Maybe she did."

Kate walked to the bookshelf and took down Joanna Redfield's Bible. As she returned to Anna, she paged through until she found the page she sought.

"Do you recognize this book?"

Anna's eyes lit up. "That's my mama's Bible."

"Somehow it came to be here. I'm glad, because there are things in her book you should know. Your mother has this verse circled, which means that she read it often. Listen:

'Come to me, all ye that labour and are heavy laden, and I will give you rest. Take my yoke upon you, and learn of me, for I am meek and lowly in heart: and ye shall find rest unto your souls. For my yoke is easy, and my burden is light.' Can you understand those words, Anna?" Kate asked.

"I think so. When I hurt I should pray, and God will help me. He's my friend."

Kate grinned and squeezed the child to her. "Exactly. How does that apply to your fretting over your mother and not learning in school?"

Anna shrugged, eyes downcast.

"Have you asked God to help you?"

Anna shook her head.

"Why not?" prompted Kate.

Anna looked up at Kate with large tearful eyes. "I forgot."

Kate embraced the sweet child again. "Of course, dear, we all forget." Kate searched Anna's face and asked, "But what should you do now?"

Anna's face lit up. "Just what He wants me to!"

Gently Kate prodded, "And what is that, Anna?"

Putting her finger to her cheek, she contemplated, then answered sweetly, "I tell Jesus how I hurt and ask Him to make me feel better. I know!" she exclaimed. "I'll ask Him to let my mother come back."

Kate smiled. "You are a very smart girl. Will you also ask Jesus to help you learn in school?"

Anna nodded.

"And will you tell Him that while you would love to have your mother come back, if He needs her more, you will make the best of life without her?"

"Is my mama dead?" Anna asked boldly.

Kate flinched. "I don't know. Maybe she ran into trouble and needs time to fix things. Just trust that because God loves you, He'll do whatever is best for you."

"He will, won't He?" she asked with a beautiful smile that lit up her blue eyes until they gleamed like the sea at sunrise.

"He will," Kate assured her. "Just don't forget to trust Him and talk to Him every single day."

"I promise."

"Me, too." Another voice in the room jarred the teacher and pupil.

"Josh!" Anna exclaimed. "Have you come for me already?"

"It's four o'clock. If Miss Hunter is finished with you, run out and jump into the carriage. It's Ayda's night off, so we're going to Lucy's Restaurant for dinner tonight."

"Really?" Anna flung a happy look at Kate. "See, God's making me feel better already!" She jumped up and addressed her teacher earnestly, "I love eating at Lucy's, especially the dessert!" She ran toward the door. "See you tomorrow, Miss Hunter, and I promise to learn!" She dashed out the door.

Kate smiled and shook her head. "What an inspiring young lady!"

"She is that, isn't she?" Josh's eyes sparkled with pride. "Anna is the dearest thing in my life," the wide-shouldered man whispered softly.

"I overheard some of the things you said to her. I didn't mean to eavesdrop . . . , yet once I began listening, I couldn't help myself. I liked what you told her. I've tried to say those very things to her, but they never came out the same. Thank you." The powerful, muscular man moved toward the door with surprising grace.

"Wait!" Kate called. "May I ask you a personal question?"

He gave a forced smile and a terse nod.

Kate looked at Josh Redfield pleadingly. "In the name of God, can you tell me where your wife is?"

Josh Redfield's face darkened with an unreadable emotion. "Because you've asked out of concern for Anna and not just idle curiosity or to gossip, I'll give you the most truthful answer I've given anyone yet to that question: Miss Hunter, I don't have a wife."

Before she could comprehend the meaning of his words, he was gone.

"Dear God," she moaned. "Joanna Redfield *is* dead! And Josh knows it!"

6

Kate was delighted with her pupils' fervent attitudes toward learning. Arrangements were being made for Kate to board at the Kesslers' as soon as Lydia Spencer arrived from New York. No longer did Kate dread staying with the families—except for the Grooms—for she'd now become familiar with them. The Groom children took more effort to love, because they were always soiled and often carried the odor of unwashed flesh. How could she manage to live in such a household? Kate had not met the Grooms.

Kate felt fortunate that the school kept her too busy to worry about Lydia's imminent arrival. She prayed constantly that something would prevent Geoffrey from marrying this woman. He was perfect for herself. The more she saw of him on weekends and special occasions, the more she idolized him. He was her knight in shining armor, her Prince Charming, her Ivanhoe.

Kate loved working in the shop on Saturday. She met such interesting people. One sunny, fall morning a woman who looked like a mere child came into the store. She wore her hair in one long braid, and her dress appeared old and faded, but clean.

Her fresh face smiled broadly when she saw Kate. "You must be the teacher!"

"I'm Kate Hunter." She nodded.

"My name's Clara Mullins. I don't have children old enough for your school yet—at least I don't think so. That's why I'm here. I need to find out if Randy is ready for school. All the local children are bragging about it, and he simply cannot wait!"

Kate laughed gently. "How old is Randy?"

"Just turned five last week. Harley, my husband, thought perhaps you could accept him."

"I'd have to evaluate him, but he could be ready. If you bring him out to the school on Monday before nine or after three, I'll see him."

"Thank you, Miss Hunter. Is there anything I can do to help you?" she asked sincerely.

"Please call me Kate." She gently commented, "From what Margo tells me you have your hands quite full now. How old are your babies?"

"Randy, the oldest, is five. Nancy will be four tomorrow; Emmet is three; Eleanor is fifteen months; and our newest is yet to come." She patted her prominent stomach.

"I hadn't even noticed." Kate blushed.

"Thank you!" She smiled proudly. "Are you certain there isn't anything I can do for you?"

"There is one thing—but I hate to ask." Kate faltered, knowing that her request was wrong. "Your mother works for the Redfields, doesn't she?"

Clara nodded.

"Anna, one of my best pupils, is having problems due to

what happened at home. I wondered if your mother could shed any light on what happened to Joanna Redfield. I'm not prying for the sake of gossip, you understand. I'm sincerely concerned for Anna."

Clara looked at her sympathetically. "I've heard about your devotion to your students, and I wish I could help you. However, my mother never speaks of these things. She won't say a word either way—even to me. It's not that she means to be difficult—"

"I understand." Kate thought she really *did* understand, for guilt at even mentioning the subject coursed through her. After all, Anna had become a model student, and only the fear that her habits might return had given Kate an excuse to ask. Her guilt intensified at the sight of her next customer.

As Clara Mullins opened the shop door to leave, balancing a large chocolate cake, Josh Redfield appeared and held the door open for her. She and Josh greeted each other amicably enough to dispel Kate's fear of trouble that recurred whenever Joshua Redfield appeared on the scene.

Walking slowly to where Kate counted cookies and bundled them into dozens, he greeted her almost shyly. "Miss Hunter. . . ." He stopped when she turned at the sound of his voice.

"How are you this fine morning, Mr. Redfield?" Kate treated him as she would any other customer. After all, hadn't Margo asked her to give him a fair chance?

His eyes took on a sheen of purpose. "I'm fine, thank you." He cleared his throat nervously. "I don't know everything you said to Anna the other day, but ever since, she's been steadily improving. In fact, she's almost her old, normal self!"

Friendly, smiling, chatting in a relaxed manner, as she'd

never seen him, Kate realized Josh Redfield was quite handsome in a rugged way. But as soon as she remembered who he was, his good looks seemed to vanish.

He must have sensed the change in her. "I merely stopped in to tell you and thank you." He gave her a brief nod and walked briskly out of the shop.

Kate had barely recuperated from Josh's visit when Jane Kessler swung gaily into the shop, carrying a package. " 'Morning, Kate."

"Good morning. How are you, Mrs. Kessler?"

"*Jane*, please! You make me feel ancient." Before Kate could respond, Jane pushed the package at her. "Here, I've brought you a gift. Go on," she coaxed. "Open it, I made it myself."

Kate untied the string in stunned silence. A gift! How exciting! Unraveling the paper carefully, Kate peeked within. Slowly she withdrew a beautiful, high-necked, black-and-gold-striped satin dress. Kate gasped with delight.

"Oh! Jane! It's the loveliest dress I've ever seen! How can I repay you? I've never owned such a delicately sewn dress! Your work is excellent!"

Jane blushed, smiling proudly, "I'd seen one similar to it on the governor's wife, back in Philadelphia. When I saw you, I knew it would be perfect for you, so I got to work."

Kate sighed with delight. "But where can I wear it, here in Kansas?"

"The holidays will soon be upon us. It would be perfect for Christmas."

Kate hugged Jane warmly and reminded herself, *There's always the wedding.*

"A big crowd's gathered down by the square," Jane said.

"Someone important must have come to town. I couldn't see much as I came in, except quite a few welcomers around the noon stage and an awful lot of luggage strapped to the top." Jane chuckled. "Whoever it is doesn't travel light."

"Hays is expecting a new editor for the newspaper. Perhaps it's he," offered Kate. "Maybe he brought his family, or at least his wife, with all that luggage!"

Just then, the twins burst through the shop door. "Miss Hunter," cried Carl breathlessly, "where's Ma?"

Earl ran toward the kitchen door, "Ma! Come quick! She's here!"

Jane and Kate exchanged confused looks.

"Boys!" scolded Kate. "Calm down and tell us *who* is here."

While Earl dashed into the kitchen, Carl stayed and explained. "Miss Spencer! It's Miss Spencer who's here! Mr. Grandville sent us to get Ma, quick."

Kate's throat tightened. "I see. Goodness, I thought the queen of England herself had just ridden in on the stage!"

Margo threw her apron at Kate as she raced through the store, toward the door. "Thanks, Kate! I'll be right back!"

When the shop quieted again, Kate looked sadly at Jane. "Well, looks as if I'll be moving in with your family soon."

"We can hardly wait!" Jane beamed. "In fact, we have so much room at our house, I don't know why you couldn't stay with us the whole school year."

Kate looked at her hopefully. "Would the school district allow that?"

"I'll speak to O'Brien myself, though I don't see why we can't," said Jane.

Kate examined her dress carefully. "Where did you learn to sew so expertly?"

"My father is a tailor in Philadelphia. He came to this

country from Warsaw. At age ten he and his brothers were sent to different homes to learn trades. My father, Tom, apprenticed with a tailor, his brother Walter learned the hotel business, and my uncle John is a barber. After their apprenticeships, they came to America, settled in Pittsburgh, then Philadelphia, and slowly worked their way into businesses of their own."

"And he taught you! What a wonderful gift from your father!"

Jane nodded. "I feel especially blessed, but after years of reading the Bible, Mr. Kessler and I have discovered that we've been very selfish with our gifts. So whenever I can, I create a special outfit, like this dress, and give it to someone. This is my way of sharing the gifts from both my earthly and heavenly fathers: The gift of sewing and the gift of love."

"How beautiful," sighed Kate, wondering wildly if she had one. "Does God give everyone a gift?"

"I can only tell you what we learned from a traveling preacher last year. Whenever Ben Hanson comes to this area, he stays with us. He always preaches on God's gifts. He quotes Romans twelve frequently, something about each of us having different gifts from God and our using them. I don't recall it word for word." She laughed lightly. "Though I should: He's quoted it enough."

"I'll read it later. I never thought about having a gift that I could use for Him." Maybe teaching was hers—didn't she give that to others?

"I recall Ben saying 'If you don't know what your gift is, ask, and He'll show you.' Well, I knew immediately what my gift was." Jane bowed her head. "I also know my shortcoming."

"Shortcoming?" Kate looked at her blankly.

"Oh, yes! As well as being gifted, we all have our weak place. He called it our 'Achilles heel.' Ben says Satan knows this area and uses it to pull us away from God."

"Really?" Kate's eyes widened. "I've never heard such things." She wondered what her Achilles heel was.

"Mine is gossip. Whenever I hear it, my ears perk up, and it isn't long before my ears relay it to my lips, and I'm caught with my foot in my mouth. Like the day I met you. It wasn't Martha's fault. She merely blurted out what she'd heard me tell Mr. Kessler about Olive Groom's housekeeping. Fine example I set for my daughter! It's moments like that when we realize how human we are. I must overcome that weakness—if not for myself, for my children."

Jane had left Kate with several things to ponder, yet she wasn't afforded the time to do so, for in moments the shop was filled with people: Margo, Geoffrey, Reginald Safford, Mitchell Hadden, Luther Aldrich, and a young woman.

Kate's eyes flew immediately to Lydia Spencer and studied her. She smiled to herself. *So this is the woman Geoffrey wants to marry?* Kate had pictured her as beautiful and sophisticated.

Lydia was plain, plump, and dressed frumpishly. *What, thought Kate, would attract an aristocratic man like Geoffrey, used to the fine ladies of London, to a woman who has no sense of dress?*

Introduced to her, Kate had to admit the other woman immediately responded with a warm, loving smile that lighted up her face and made her look almost pretty.

All right, Kate admitted. *Geoffrey probably knows she has a charming smile, but will that last when they marry? Can it take away the sting of knowing your wife never looks her best?*

When all the commotion had calmed down and Elmer

had carried in Lydia's many bags, Margo pulled Kate aside. "I need to speak to you," she whispered.

Kate nodded.

"I'm sorry, but we'll need your room sooner than I'd thought. . . ." Margo tried to explain.

Lydia approached them and interrupted earnestly, "No. I won't hear of Kate giving up her room because of me. Is the room large enough? We'll share it."

Taken by surprise, Margo hesitated. "I suppose it is—"

"Good. Then Kate and I will be shipmates!" Lydia exclaimed with childlike excitement. "If that's acceptable to you, that is, Kate?" Lydia gazed at her expectantly.

Kate felt cornered and suddenly confused. How could she politely object? Everyone would think she was horrid if she turned down such a friendly, generous offer. *Yet how could I possibly room with the girl who is engaged to the man I love?* she wondered uncomfortably.

"You know," remarked Margo, "that would work out just fine, if you girls don't mind being cramped—for a week at the most." She turned to Kate. "Would you stay at least another week, to teach Lydia the running of the store? The only way Lydia will accept our hospitality is if we let her work for her keep." Margo winked. "I know exactly how to keep you busy; don't I, Kate?"

"Yes, but it's fun. I've enjoyed every minute of it."

"Then I'm sure I shall, too," agreed the rosy-cheeked Lydia.

"I hope you won't be too busy for me?" Geoffrey walked over and put his arm about his betrothed's waist. "I can't believe you're finally here—and early, too!"

Lydia smiled coyly.

"How do you like the West, so far?" he asked.

"Truthfully?" she asked, a worried look in her eyes.

"Naturally," Geoffrey laughed.

Lydia's mouth trembled slightly, her ever-ready smile faded, and her hand flew to her mouth. "Oh! It's horrid here! How can I ever learn to stand the dirt, the emptiness, and all those rough men?" Her eyes darted for a quick escape, but in this strange house, she didn't know where to flee. Her face took on a look of panic, before large tears tumbled from her large eyes.

"Sweetheart!" Geoffrey cried, reaching out for her.

Seeing Lydia's dilemma, Kate naturally jumped into action; without hesitation, she grabbed Lydia's hand and pulled her briskly from the room. Kate called over her shoulder, "We'll be down in plenty of time for lunch. We need time to freshen up, is all."

7

*O*pening the door to the bedroom, Kate stood frozen in momentary shock. Crates and suitcases crammed the space. Wherever would they both find room? What on earth had this girl brought with her?

Lydia swayed in Kate's grasp.

"Are you all right? Lydia?" Kate asked, truly concerned.

The other woman sniffled, blew her nose, pocketed her handkerchief, and forced a smile. "I'm fine. Just tired from traveling, I guess. Only let me lie down for a few minutes and rest."

Kate closed the window drapes and helped Lydia to the large double bed. "Lie down and be still for a while. I'll get a wet cloth for your head."

Skirting a mountain of luggage, Kate went to the pitcher, on the dresser, poured cold water onto a washcloth, and placed it on the woman's forehead.

Lydia took Kate's hand. "You're so kind. Thank you, too, for getting me out of that embarrassing situation. The moment I saw you, I knew we'd be friends, because I felt you were a kindred spirit."

Kate could hardly understand why she felt sympathy for this strange girl and her predicament, but she responded, "Glad I was on hand. Just close your eyes and rest. I'll sit in the rocking chair and read, if the lamp light won't bother you."

"Surely it won't," she said. "And thank you again."

Kate made herself comfortable in the old rocker and flipped to her marked place in the romantic novel she was reading, *Martha's Secret Tryst.*

"Kate . . . ," Lydia's voice called weakly.

"Yes."

"I don't know what I'd have done without you."

"Oh, I'm sure in a few days you'll wish I'd hurry and leave. I'll get on your nerves that fast!"

Lydia seemed silent awfully long, then Kate heard her murmur before falling fast asleep, "No, I don't think you will."

At lunch and later at dinner, Lydia was her old happy-go-lucky self. She laughed, held hands with Geoffrey, and chattered at Kate. Cringing within herself, Kate's saving thoughts were Lydia's words of truth about the West that morning: *"Oh! it's horrid here!"* Would Lydia decide to go back East, leaving Geoffrey free? Kate's conscience squirmed.

After dinner she studied the couple as they enjoyed dessert. Geoffrey spooned mincemeat pie into Lydia's mouth, while she protested that he gave her too much. They giggled and shared intimate gazes.

What does he see in her? Kate contrasted her own petite, firm, slim form with the other woman's plump figure.

Could Kate's charming face with high cheekbones give way before a moon-shaped one that creased when she smiled, instead of dimpling? Yet Geoffrey seemed to prefer pin-straight, dull hair to her own naturally curling, radiant locks.

However, Kate's better nature admitted Lydia's large brown eyes and sparkling smile had their attractions.

Look at her expensive clothes! a little voice insisted. *But they do nothing for her shape, and she doesn't have much sense of color.* When she arrived, Kate remembered, Lydia had worn a dark-blue skirt with a black blouse; tonight's outfit, a brown skirt and matching jacket with a mud-gray blouse, made Kate flinch.

After the fine ways of the English gentry, how could such things fail to matter to Geoffrey?

It's not that I don't like Lydia, Kate mused. *Of course I do, but I don't want her and Geoffrey to be unhappy. Can they be meant for each other, when they have such different attitudes? Could I live with myself if I never warned them?* But at the thought of confronting either party, Kate's courage failed. *Maybe I could simply help them find out for themselves.*

As she turned away, Kate felt uncomfortable. What had come over her, thinking that way?

Before climbing into bed for the night, Kate, Margo, and Lydia shared hot cocoa. The three, dressed in nightgowns, sat upon the bed, like young schoolgirls.

Margo and Lydia chatted excitedly about her spring wedding, while Kate tried to imagine what it would be like to marry Geoffrey.

During a lull in the conversation, Lydia surprised Kate by asking, "What about you, Kate? Is there anyone special in your life?"

Kate froze, stunned by the question. "M-me? No. No one special yet." She recovered herself and continued, "There were a few men back East I liked, but never anyone I loved or wanted to marry."

"What about Geoffrey's friends?" Lydia suggested.

"His friends?" Kate blinked blankly.

"Why, yes. Reginald Safford and Mitchell whatever-his-name-is. Both are extremely handsome, don't you think?"

If Lydia thought Reginald and Mitchell were attractive, perhaps she would be happier with one of them. Kate answered with this thought in mind. "They are, aren't they? I'll keep them both in mind." Kate winked. "But just now I'm concentrating on my school and pupils, and that keeps me busy."

Margo stood up, hands on hips. "Kate, you're constantly buried in romantic books. Are you saying you aren't at all interested in finding your Prince Charming?"

"Sure, but I'm in no rush."

Lydia flew to her friend's defense. "We should mind our own business. It's just that I'm so happy with Geoffrey that I wish I could share it with you. Of course that isn't possible. When the time is right, you'll have your own 'Geoffrey.' "

Kate smiled mischievously. "I'm sure I will."

The next morning Kate began training Lydia to work in the store. While she had a hard time remembering prices, Lydia excelled in making change. Business was slow that day, so in their free time the two women became better acquainted.

"Working in the store is fun," remarked Lydia.

"Time goes fast, too. It's almost lunchtime," reminded Kate.

"Yesterday at this time I was in tears," Lydia sulked.

"You certainly took me by surprise," admitted Kate. "How you can be so cheerful one moment and a tearful wreck the next, I don't know. What made you so upset?"

"I couldn't believe the stage driver when he said this was Hays City. Coming from New York, I guess the word *city* caused me to picture something quite different. When we drove across the plains, with nothing in sight for miles, I felt so insecure and terribly small. I'm used to buildings and neighbors all around me. The more the merrier! To me, Hays City seems the end of the world."

"Do you want to leave, then?" Kate ventured.

"Certainly not."

"But why, when you seem to hate it?" Lydia now had Kate totally baffled.

"The man I love has made his home here. He has asked me to share that life. I accepted, gave my word that I would. No matter what, I'll have to make the best of it!"

Secretly Kate envied the girl's loyalty and determination.

"You seem to have adjusted nicely," said Lydia. "So shall I."

"But *I* didn't come from a big city. I lived on a farm outside of Chicago. I'm used to desolation, to some extent."

Lydia smiled placidly. "As long as Geoffrey is here, I'll learn to like it. Besides, I know I can count on you to help me. Right, Kate?"

With a slight frown, Kate replied with little enthusiasm, "Sure." She was glad a customer came in just then and interrupted the conversation. Couldn't Lydia see there was nothing she could do to help her? No city woman belonged here.

Later that same day, Kate met Georgie Plumb's mother for the first time. Just before she and Lydia closed the shop, to make deliveries, a thin, overly made-up woman entered the store and approached Lydia.

"Are you the teacher?" she asked in a raspy voice.

"No, Kate's the teacher," Lydia said, pointing to her.

Extending one hand, Kate smiled. "I'm Kate Hunter."

"Nice to meet ya. I'm Fannie Plumb, Georgie's mother. How's he doin', anyway?" She shook Kate's hand heartily.

"Well, I'm glad you asked, because I've had some problems with your son. He's smart enough, but his deportment is lacking."

"Deport—What?" she asked.

"His behavior in class. He's constantly disrupting the other children and making unkind comments. Perhaps you could speak to him about this?"

"I'll have his pa beat his backside 'til it's raw," she spat.

"Oh, no!" exclaimed Kate. "Don't do that! Couldn't you simply have a talk with him?"

"Sure, but he don't listen. The boy is goin' through that problem age, ya know?"

Kate nodded. "I have a brother myself." Straightening her apron, she asked, "What can we get for you today?"

"I need a special dessert for dinner tonight; it's our wedding anniversary."

"Wonderful! How many years?" asked Kate.

"Ten. Ten long years. And not all have been pleasant, either! But we stuck it out, no matter what. That's more than I can say for some around here. My George drinks some, but he's a good man. It's just harder to see the good when he's been drinkin'.

"I'll never give up on him, though. Not like them Redfields. George is sure there must have been foul play there. Especially after he heard that argument between Phillip

Barringer and Redfield the day before Joanna's disappearance."

"Argument?" Kate asked, curious despite herself.

"Yep. George heard them yellin' at each other, right in front of the lumberyard. George didn't catch what Phillip yelled at Josh, but he heard Josh's reply as clear as yer hearin' me. Redfield shook his fist at Phillip and said, 'You'll leave with her, over my dead body!' "

Kate's mouth fell open. "*Josh* said that?"

"As sure as I'm standin' here! And I see Josh is still alive, so I'm wonderin' how Barringer managed to escape with Joanna. Could it have been over *their* dead bodies?"

Kate gasped. "Mrs. Plumb, you mustn't say such things."

The woman frowned. "I'm sick of holdin' my tongue. Why should men like Josh Redfield get away with anything? If one of *us* did something illegal, we'd hang; yet the sheriff doesn't do anything to *him*."

"Perhaps he needs more evidence," Kate offered lamely.

"How much more does he need? They found Joanna's wedding ring, which she never removed. She left her most precious possession behind, her daughter. This argument proves there was friction between them. What's the law waiting for?" She shook her head. "Poor little Anna."

"Yes," murmured Kate. "Poor little Anna."

"Who is Redfield?" Lydia asked when Fannie Plumb had left.

"Josh Redfield is the father of one of my pupils," Kate replied from her deep thoughtfulness.

"Did he do something dreadful?"

"Everyone thinks he did."

"Do you?"

71

Kate shook her head. "I don't know what to think. Better not mention it to Margo, she detests gossip."

"I won't," Lydia said obediently.

"C'mon." Kate changed the subject. "Let's pack up all the orders and leftovers and make our evening rounds."

"Evening rounds?"

"The restaurants and a few other establishments here in Hays order fresh bread and baked goods at regular price and buy our leftovers for half price. We always save something for the Mullins family, too."

"I wouldn't have thought a bakery could do so well in a town where many don't have much money. Don't most of the women have to do their own baking?" Lydia asked, wrapping the baked goods as Kate showed her.

"I didn't think so, either, but actually they do quite well. If they had to depend solely on the individual families, I suppose they wouldn't show much profit. The restaurants, hotels, and the few rich families make this business thrive. The families from Victoria buy almost all their goods from the bake shop."

"Victoria? Isn't that where Geoffrey and I will live?"

"I believe so."

"The women don't bake? But why?" Lydia asked.

"They don't have time, I suppose."

"What do they do?"

"Play tennis, polo, and have fox hunts," Kate replied with a touch of sarcasm.

"What about the farming and chores?"

"They claim that if they all pitch in and do the work together, they can get it done in less time. Most of the other settlers around here just shake their heads at them. Many say they'll only last a year. According to Mr. Kessler, it's impossible for them to survive on the small, neglected gardens they plant.

"A local came in one day and asked Margo how long the Victorians' money would last! They buy everything. The Victorian women keep the general store in business, too, because they buy all their clothes and other essentials."

Lydia laughed. "Why don't they just live in the city, then?"

"Because the land agent made this Kansas property sound so good, they invested. Now they're trying to show they can succeed where regular people cannot, using money instead of hard work."

Kate added, "I must say one thing in defense of the Victorians. They are sure making the businesses in Hays profitable. Without them and their money. . . . You see, the other pioneers buy only bare necessities. They grow all their own food and make their clothing, except for an occasional treat or special occasion."

"Yet the Victorians are not failing as pioneers?" Lydia asked.

"While other pioneers packed their wagons with old clothes, tin utensils, and wooden tools, the Victorians filled their trunks with sterling and gold, silk and satin, porcelain and crystal. Instead of struggling to earn a living from our good earth, these people enjoy cricket games, banquets, and soirees. Leisure takes precedence over work. So far they've held their own, but they certainly have not thrived—off the land anyhow. They still have money and spend it freely."

"Surely their money cannot last forever?"

Kate shrugged.

Lydia perked up. "Geoffrey told me that Sir George Grant, a wealthy silk merchant, was the driving force behind the settlement. He bought fifty thousand acres of land and organized the Victorian colony."

"I heard that, too," said Kate. "Margo also told me many of the relatives of Victorians are sending them money and things such as sheep, horses, and cattle!" Kate shook her head. "If only they were willing to give up some of their social customs, they would have had the best beginning in this new world."

"Geoffrey says," Lydia said excitedly, "that one woman in Victoria actually has a piano!"

"Yes, but I'm afraid that the other settlers resent the Victorians and their ostentatiousness."

Lydia frowned. "Some women in Victoria must not buy everything and must act as true pioneers."

"You'll have to ask Geoffrey," said Kate. "I don't know."

"Oh, dear!" Lydia's eyes brightened with tears. "You don't suppose Geoffrey wants me to become a true pioneer and work my fingers to the bone?" She added quickly. "Not that I don't think it's necessary, but I wouldn't know how to start!"

"I'm sure he only expects as much from you as the other Victorian men expect of their wives," Kate said honestly.

Shaking her head vehemently, Lydia disagreed, "I don't think so. He told me to learn as much as I can from Margo. Just yesterday he said he wants me to learn domesticity!"

"Geoffrey said that?"

Lydia nodded. "He either wants me to be like the local pioneers or. . . ." She hesitated and looked about cautiously. "Or he is running out of money, and he *needs* me to be domestic."

8

Odd, Josh Redfield hasn't come for Anna yet, Kate thought, looking up from her paperwork. She watched the little girl, patiently waiting by the door in the now-empty schoolroom. Where could he be? He'd never been late before.

"Did Josh say he'd come later?" Kate asked, trying not to show too much concern, lest Anna worry.

With a forlorn look, Anna shook her head.

"I'm sure he's gotten busy at the lumberyard. I have paperwork to do anyway, and I like your company. Why don't you sit here beside me and begin reading your homework assignment?"

Anna's lower lip protruded and quivered. "Maybe Josh is gone, like my mother!" Tears filled her eyes and threatened to spill over.

"No! He's held up somewhere is all!" Kate came to Anna and embraced her. "What could happen to a big man like Josh?"

"Maybe someone kilded him. . . ."

A tear escaped down Anna's cheek, and Kate caught it with her hand. "That's *killed*, and no one would hurt Josh."

"Some people don't like him." Anna looked up at Kate. "Why?"

"Why do you think they *should* like him?" Kate tested.

"Because he's good and kind. He truly cares about everyone," Anna said positively. "He's my favoritest person in the world."

"*Most favorite*, Anna," Kate corrected.

"Do you like him?" she asked looking up at Kate with large, tearful eyes.

Kate hesitated. "I suppose I do. I never gave it much thought before. I don't *dislike* him," she felt she answered honestly enough.

"Georgie Plumb says folks think he did something bad to my mother. Do you think that, too?"

Kate flushed and suddenly felt clammy with discomfort. "I—I t-thought. . . ." Kate straightened and held her chin high. "Anna, I'll be honest with you. I did hear what folks are saying and have wondered if it's true. I don't know. Do you think Josh would hurt your mother?"

"Never! Josh wouldn't hurt anyone, especially my mother. He likes her."

"*Likes*?" queried Kate. "Surely you mean *loves*."

"Sure, loves, then. They were always nice to each other. I never heard them yell and call names, like Georgie Plumb's mama and papa do."

"You saw affection between them?" asked Kate.

"*Affection*? What do you mean?"

"Kissing? Hugging?"

Anna thought for several moments. "No, but on Christmas he kissed her on the cheek." Anna grinned. "He said he saves all his kisses and hugs for *me!*"

Kate wondered about the odd relationship they seemed to have had, then scolded herself. Many couples didn't show affection in front of their children and even referred to each other by the titles of *Mr.* and *Mrs.* The fact that Anna never saw affection proved nothing. She reminded herself to think more positively about Josh Redfield.

"I'm glad he shows so much affection to you. Did your mother seem happy?"

Anna shrugged. "Sometimes she cried in her bedroom."

"Was Josh in there with her when she cried?" Kate asked, wondering if she cried because he'd been unkind to her.

"No. Josh never went into her room."

Kate gasped. "They had separate bedrooms?"

"Oh, yes, and I have my own room, too. It's pink with—"

Kate interrupted. "Perhaps you'd better begin reading your assignment."

Anna searched Kate's face for several moments, then obeyed.

An hour later, Josh drove up to the schoolhouse, with a passenger.

Anna flew into his arms. "Josh, where were you? I was so worried."

"I'm sorry, princess, but I had to meet someone's stage, and it was late." He pointed to an elderly gentleman sitting upon the wagon bench. "This is my father, your grandfather."

Anna retreated one step, cautiously. "Grandfather?" she asked. "But . . . you said he lived in England."

"I do," a grouchy voice answered. "A man can travel, can't he?" Anna took another step away from the barking voice.

77

"No Redfield backs away from his own kin." The gruff-voiced man winked without smiling. "What's your name?"

"A-Anna. . . ."

"*Anna*. That's a good name. Jump up here by me so we can get home. I'm so hungry I could eat one of these horses!"

Despite his gruff tone, a soft quality peeked through the toughness, and Anna felt his harmlessness.

"You'd have to cook them first," she replied.

"This heat could cook anything!" he snapped.

Anna looked up at him and smiled. "It can't."

He ruffled her hair. "Then I'll eat them raw!" His eyes twinkled. "Joshua, are we going to stand here all day?"

Josh stepped forward. "I wanted you to meet Anna's teacher, Miss Hunter. Miss Hunter, this is my father, from London, Arthur Redfield."

Kate nodded and smiled. As the wagon rolled toward the back of the schoolhouse and the new Redfield home, she waved to Anna. When they'd gone, Kate sighed. She didn't know what to make of the Redfields.

Looking off into the distance, Kate could see the dust of an approaching wagon and called loudly to the twins, who had been playing in the fields behind the schoolhouse since lessons had ended. That would be Margo to pick them up.

Kate remained silent on the way home, as the trip was too noisy to allow conversation. The twins played in the back of the wagon, and the horses' galloping hooves drowned out voices. She thought about Anna and their talk. What had she learned about the Redfields? That Anna's parents hadn't been very affectionate and that Josh Redfield loved Anna very much. What else? He was fond of Joanna, yet not openly affectionate, and they had separate rooms?

Kate thought she'd figured out old Mr. Redfield. He was

a gruff, grouchy old man who had great capacity for love but felt it best to keep his emotions hidden. Maybe he thought his sensitivity a handicap rather than an asset?

When they reached home and the shop, Kate cringed at the sight of Geoffrey's horse tethered out front. Hadn't her day been hectic enough? How could she face watching him with Lydia?

During dinner, when Lydia and Geoffrey weren't absorbed in each other too intently, Kate's news won her everyone's attention.

"An interesting person came into town today," she announced calmly.

"Really," said Margo, who stopped spooning her soup. "Who?"

Enjoying the center stage, Kate merely smiled.

"Do tell us, Kate," prodded Geoffrey. "No one will eat another bite until you do."

"I know," said Lydia. "The newspaper editor has finally arrived."

"He may have," stalled Kate. "But that isn't the person I'm thinking of."

"Would you be so kind as to tell us, Kate, so we can enjoy our dinner?" asked Elmer with raised eyebrows and an indulgent smile.

"Please, Kate," pleaded Margo. "This town is boring enough to drive us all crazy. We need a diversion. Who is our visitor?"

"Someone's father came in on the afternoon stage, all the way from London, England!"

"*London!*" they all echoed at once.

"A relative of someone in Victoria?" Geoffrey asked.

Kate shook her head. "No. Josh Redfield's father, Arthur."

Margo gasped. "No! Really! He's here already?"

"You knew he was coming, then?" Kate asked.

"Josh said he would be coming as soon as the railroad opened. Strange he couldn't wait," Margo said.

Kate shrugged. "He seems awfully grouchy. He didn't smile once and scared his own granddaughter."

Margo nodded knowingly. "Josh told me that his disposition isn't pleasant and never has been. Yet Josh seems to revere him. He is his father, after all." Margo offered everyone more bread from a decorative basket. "Honor thy father and mother; . . . and thou mayest live long on the earth."

Kate spoke without thinking. "Do you suppose, then, that Joanna didn't honor her parents?"

"Kate!" scolded Margo.

She immediately regretted the statement, until Geoffrey winked at her and smiled.

"Did Josh say why his father was here?" Kate asked Margo. "I mean, is it for business or pleasure?"

Elmer spoke at last, "You know, he did mention something, and it was before Joanna left, too! He told me after one of the education meetings that his father was coming from England to help him and Joanna settle a family problem. When I asked him if it was anything serious, he laughed nervously and said, 'No, just a family difficulty that took place in England and needs to be straightened out at last.' "

"Elmer . . . ," Margo said in a warning tone.

"Wonder what he meant?" Kate asked, gazing off into space, her imagination running. "I know! There was probably an argument between Josh's family and Joanna's or between Arthur and Joanna. Perhaps they left England in anger. Do you think Arthur forbade them to marry or something? He may have had a rich lady picked out for Josh to marry."

"Kate!" Margo exclaimed. "Wherever did you get such an imagination? I think you're on the wrong side of your books! You should write them!"

"But it's possible, isn't it?" she pleaded.

Margo shrugged. "Anything is possible."

"Actually," put in Geoffrey, "Josh is a convicted criminal who escaped from a ship bound for Australia. Arthur is the law, bringing him back to hang!"

"Geoffrey!" Lydia scolded. "That isn't the story at all. I have the real story."

"You do?" Geoffrey cuffed her chin. "Tell us!"

"Joshua and Joanna refused to live with such an ornery old coot and eloped to America. The father has finally tracked them down. I'll bet he brought all his luggage and plans to stay forever."

Everyone laughed, including Kate, yet she felt hurt by their remarks. She'd been serious. Had they thought her joking? When the truth came out, they'd apologize.

Kate packed her clothes without regret. She'd missed her privacy and couldn't even curl up with a good book without Lydia's constantly asking questions. The other woman always wanted to talk, and sometimes Kate needed to be alone.

Besides, watching the love blossom between Lydia and Geoffrey was painful.

At first, looking back on the things they'd shared, Kate thought Geoffrey was certain to notice how much they had in common. How could he fail to understand how unsuited he and Lydia were? But one night at dinner, she saw the spark in Geoffrey's eyes when he glanced at Lydia and the intense gaze that followed.

He's never looked at me that way, Kate thought sorrowfully. *We shared some fun, but he's never looked after me as if I were a treasure. Why, that's the way he treats Lydia!* Then she realized that in the last few days Geoffrey had hardly seemed to know that she, Kate, was alive.

I still don't think they're suited. Kate tried to bolster up her hopes. *Maybe all it needs is time.* Yet her heart only felt tight with pain.

Well, she'd taught Lydia the store work; now she could leave and board with the Kesslers. Yanking another drawer out and carefully transferring clothes from it to the suitcase, Kate didn't hear anyone enter.

"Leaving us already?" Margo asked sadly.

Putting on a pleasant smile, Kate replied, "It's time."

"Perhaps not."

"What do you mean? You asked me to stay a week and teach Lydia the store. I did that! The Kesslers expect me." Kate shut the drawer and closed her suitcase.

"True, but something may have changed that." Margo looked around the cramped bedroom. "I'm sorry for this past week. You must have felt awfully crowded. If only I had something better to offer you!"

"What's happened?"

"Measles. Randy Mullins got it a few days ago, and Ella Kessler broke out this morning. Nancy Balcomb stopped by and offered to take you into their home next, but it might be risky for you. Peter and Ella sit beside each other in class and are close friends. He may be next. We're afraid of an epidemic. Mr. O'Brien told Joshua Redfield that he would formally close the school until the sickness had abated."

"That explains why Clara Mullins never stopped by the school with Randy. You heard all this just now?"

"By degrees, this morning. Everyone who came in had news or comments."

"Has anyone else come down with it?" Concern for her pupils overtook Kate's personal troubles.

"So far just Randy, Ella, and Mary Jane Haun."

"Thanks be to God!"

"Yes, and I asked Doc Evans to check the twins. He said he'd be over this afternoon."

Kate sighed and looked about the cramped room that had once seemed a sanctuary. "Then I must stay here, right?"

"Actually you've two other offers, but you are welcome to turn them both down and stay here. In fact Lydia asked me to beg you to stay. She's awfully fond of you." Margo smoothed her apron. "Please consider staying."

"Thank you for wanting me." Kate smiled warmly. "But surely I need to consider the other offers, too."

Margo gave Kate a warning look and said quickly, "The Grooms."

"Oh!" she exclaimed in reflex to the name. "I'm not sure I can. . . . And the other?" she asked, knowing she'd accept it, no matter whom it was.

Margo fidgeted before blurting, "The Redfields."

9

"*T*he Redfields?" Kate said in disbelief. "But how can they invite me? No woman lives in their home. Would that be proper?"

"The housekeeper lives in, and Josh's father is there now, so it is quite acceptable. They have a respectable household. A Christian home, too, I might add."

"*Christian* home?" Kate uttered. "How could someone who—"

"Kate! You're judging again," Margo reminded.

"But he—"

"He what? Just what *facts* do you know about Joshua Redfield?" She held up her hand as Kate began to speak. "On your own, Kate. Not what you've heard about him, what you know to be true yourself."

Kate stopped short. She thought for several moments and decided Margo deserved an honest answer. "All right. I know he loves Anna, and she loves him. I know that he spends a lot of time with her and that he has been supportive in the town's educational pursuits and donated his time and money to the school. He goes to church and. . . ." She hesitated, looking Margo squarely in the eye. "And he has never given me reason to think any of the gossip could be true. I apologize."

"So Kate, give me one good reason why you should not accept his most generous invitation. Don't forget, either, that he lives just minutes from the schoolhouse and that Anna needs you as much as you need a place to stay just now."

Kate cast her eyes downward. "You're right. I'll accept Mr. Redfield's invitation."

Elmer carried Kate's bags into the Redfield home while she gazed up at the pillared mansion. Margo slid her arm around Kate's and prodded. "C'mon, you'll love it here."

"It looks so huge. I'll get lost for sure."

"Nonsense. Anna will shadow your every step." Margo pulled her gently toward the large double doors. "God will protect you, no matter where you live, if you ask Him."

Kate smiled. "I'll miss the store."

"The store will miss you, too!"

"But you have Lydia to take my place." She looked up at Margo. "Who is there to take *your* place? Whom can I trust here?"

"Ayda Simcox, Clara Mullins's mother," Margo stated.

Kate nodded. "From what I hear of her, she seems trustworthy. But you always say we should judge for ourselves, so I guess I'll just have to find out that way."

Margo opened one of the large double doors. "What have I been telling you about gossiping? You know she can be trusted because she has a reputation for not indulging in hearsay. Isn't that how you'd like others to think about you?"

Kate smiled, stepping into the large, tiled foyer. "I'm beginning to understand exactly how dangerous gossip is, even if you're only a listener."

She looked around the richly furnished living room, beyond the entry area. The space seemed endless, with a spiral staircase on one side and an entry into the dining room on the other. The carpet felt rich and thick when she lightly stepped on it.

A handsome-looking woman walked briskly toward them from the dining room. Her appearance gave Kate the impression of complete capability. Efficiency, exactness, and confidence exuded from her. Kate knew this had to be Mrs. Simcox, even before Margo introduced them.

She nodded abruptly, but her smile was warm and genuine. "Welcome to Hannah House, Miss Hunter."

"*Hannah House?*" Kate and Margo asked in unison.

Ayda smiled. "I have to get used to it myself; it's only been a short time since I was told. Mr. Redfield named the home, in English fashion, just before his father arrived from London. He named it for his mother, Hannah Redfield, who died when he and his sister were quite young."

"How fortunate his mother had such a beautiful name," Kate said.

"Ha!" The sound came from the direction of the front door behind them, "Hortense House wouldn't quite do, would it?"

They spun around to face old Mr. Redfield, leaning on his cane, dressed for riding.

"Mr. Redfield," Ayda scolded. "You must stop entering rooms like that. My poor heart won't last!"

"Who's Hortense?" Kate asked, looking at the old man with puzzlement.

"That's a girl I almost married!" He laughed. "Lucky for Joshua I didn't."

Kate smiled. "If I named a house after my mother, it would be *Lovinia House.*"

"That doesn't sound too bad; how about you?" Arthur Redfield pointed his cane at Margo.

"I'm sorry," Ayda interrupted. "This is Mrs. Dutton, and this is—"

"How do you do, Mrs. Dutton. I know who that is; that's Kate Hunter, the new schoolteacher. How could I not know? Isn't she all my granddaughter talks about?" He bowed curtly. "Well?" He asked again, looking at Margo, "How about your home, if it were named for your mother?"

Margo grinned. "Bertha House!"

"I certainly hope no one names a house for me," laughed Ayda. "Ayda House!"

They all roared with laughter until another voice startled them. "What is going on?" Josh said, coming down from upstairs. "Overnight my house becomes a theater." He smiled. "Welcome to Hannah House, Kate. You've met Ayda?"

Kate nodded. "Thank you."

"Why don't you show them to Kate's room, Ayda," he suggested, "while I beat my father at checkers. It won't take long. We'll be finished in plenty of time for dinner."

Kate and Margo followed Ayda up the spiral staircase to a landing with a long hall to the right. Down the dark corridor, lit only by one small wall lamp, Kate could see several highly polished mahogany doors. Stopping at the last one on the left, Ayda opened it and stood aside. "I hope this is comfortable. If you need anything, anything at all, my room is here." She pointed to the closed door right across the hall.

"Thank you, Ayda. Go inside and start unpacking, Kate. I'd like a few words with Ayda before I leave," said Margo.

When they disappeared inside the housekeeper's room, Kate closed her door and looked about.

She had never seen a bedroom shaped like this one. The outside wall was an arc and so was the window within the curved brick wall. She looked out and saw that the room was towerlike. The curved windows gave the room enough light to read by during the day, and that sunlit quality made the room feel warm, cozy, and cheerful. Kate loved her round bedroom.

Another door opened into a walk-in closet, lined in cedar. On the straight wall opposite the curved windows, on a dais, stood a large bed with ruffly bedspread and canopy. Kate leaned her head on the large wooden bedpost and sighed, "A room built for a princess."

Her door opened, and she spun around. "Oh, Margo," she exclaimed. "Look at this room! Pinch me, for I think I'm dreaming."

Margo looked all about. "Magnificent. It was Joanna's room. Does that bother you?"

"Joanna's?" she asked, looking about again. "No, I suppose not," she murmured, somewhat subdued. "After all, it isn't as if she died here or anything."

"She isn't dead at all, Kate."

"You're *sure*?" Kate questioned, shocked that Margo seemed to know more than she did. "What makes you say that?"

"Who would have killed her? Certainly not Joshua. It couldn't have been Phillip Barringer, because he's disappeared, too. I'm afraid the only story I believe is the one Josh tells. For whatever reason, Joanna has run away."

Kate looked doubtful. "I wish I knew for sure."

"Then believe it." Margo smiled. "And enjoy your stay here."

"I shall anyway," Kate said, rubbing her hand across the richly polished furniture. "I shall."

Margo walked over to the closet and opened the door. "This closet is about the size of the room you and Lydia shared."

"I know." Kate joined her. "I'll never fill it up with my meager wardrobe."

"They must have cleaned out Joanna's things in a hurry to make room for you. Wonder where they stored them all?" Margo said, running her hand along the shelf over the hanging rod. "No dust."

"Look here," Kate said pointing to three drawers built into the closet wall. "I can hide my personal things. . . ." She halted and pointed to the floor. "Is that yours?" A shiny, heart-shaped object lay on the hardwood floor, near the chest.

Margo's hand flew to the charm hanging from the chain around her neck. "No. I have mine." She bent over and picked up the small piece of jewelry. "It's a locket!"

Kate gasped. "Do you think it's Joanna's?"

Margo looked thoughtful. "The initials engraved on it are JMR, so it must be. I recall her wearing something like this at one of the meetings. It kept reflecting from the lamps and shining."

"Can we open it?" Kate asked.

"Why not?" Margo opened the locket, and they both peered at it blankly. "I suppose if we took it over by the window, we'd see better."

They walked to the windows and examined the pictures within the locket.

"That's Arthur Redfield!" exclaimed Kate. "But who is the woman?"

Margo shrugged. "Not Joanna."

"You're sure it's her locket?"

"It looks like hers. The initials begin with a J and end with an R. Who else could it have belonged to?"

"But why would she have a picture of her father-in-law and some woman in her locket?"

Margo turned the locket over in her hand. "I don't know, Kate." She handed it to her. "You keep it. Maybe Anna will know who the woman is."

Kate carefully placed the heart inside the top drawer of the bedside table. "Will you stay and help me unpack?"

Margo smiled. "Certainly. That's why I'm here." She shook her finger at Kate. "Don't think you'll be rid of me by moving, for I'll visit you often, count on it!"

"Do you think I'll still see. . . ." Kate stopped. She couldn't ask if she'd see Geoffrey. What would Margo think? "The others," she finished. "You know, Elmer, Carl, Earl, Lydia, and Geoffrey." That sounded better, she decided.

Margo gave her a sweet, motherly smile. "My! You did take to my family, didn't you?" She sighed. "I wish I'd had another room. . . ."

Kate fidgeted with discomfort. Some of it was true, she told herself. She did like Elmer and the twins. But she'd not miss them. She would miss seeing Geoffrey. How would she ever win him from here?

"Margo," she said with determination, "there's something I'd like to discuss with you while we unpack." As they began putting clothes into drawers, Kate continued, "It's about Lydia and Geoffrey. They're making a big mistake."

"How's that?" Margo asked, paying little attention.

"They are wrong for each other."

Margo suddenly gave Kate her full attention. "Wrong for each other? What do you mean, Kate?"

Kate suddenly wished she'd planned this conversation instead of plunging into it. "I'm fond of both of them and can see they are not well matched for marriage."

"Why ever not?" Margo asked, shocked by Kate's admission.

"Lydia's a wonderful young woman, but not at all for Geoffrey. He needs someone sophisticated, cultured and . . . and. . . ." She fumbled for the right word.

"Kate! What's wrong with Lydia? I thought you liked her?"

"I *do* like her. But she isn't what I'd pictured for Geoffrey."

Margo shook her head. "But she's warm, loving, caring, and sincere, not to mention good-natured, loyal, and old-fashioned. Geoffrey loves her!"

"Could be mere infatuation, or just convenient, perhaps?"

"*Convenient*? When she had to come all the way from New York?"

"Doesn't he want someone who will become more of a pioneer's wife than the Victorian women are?"

"True, he did mention once that he didn't like the uncommitted attitude of the Victorian women—or the men, for that matter. He asked me to teach her things, but he would have had me teach anyone. I wouldn't worry about Geoffrey and Lydia, Kate; they will be fine."

"Lydia will never adjust; she doesn't even like it here."

"Kate, please don't worry. It's several months before the wedding. If they aren't compatible, it will show up before then."

Kate decided further argument would be wasted on Margo. She didn't understand.

"How did he meet Lydia anyway?" she asked.

"Why, I don't know exactly. He spent a few months in New York City before coming west. I suppose he met her then," Margo said, shaking out Kate's few dresses. "Shall we hang these in the closet?"

Kate laughed. "At least we won't have to worry about their getting crushed in that mammoth closet."

After hanging the garments, Margo put her arms around Kate. "Is something else bothering you?"

Kate shook her head.

"All that concern over Lydia and Geoffrey is futile. Worry about your own Prince Charming." Margo tweaked Kate's cheeks. "Sometimes people fall in love without respect to 'types.' "

"They do?" Kate said without enthusiasm, for she still worried about never seeing Geoffrey.

"Of course. Look at Buzz and Nancy Balcomb!" Margo asked, "Can you say they're just the same?"

10

The thought of going down to dinner frightened Kate more than coming to live at Hannah House had. As she looked at her reflection in the mirror of the dressing table, she wondered how many times Joanna had stood before it, dreading something.

Kate scolded herself. Why should dining with the Redfields fill her with trepidation? Arthur's sour disposition? No. It was Josh she felt uncomfortable about. Why? Because of all she'd heard about him.

Taking the locket from the bedside table, she turned it over in her hand, wondering about Joanna. She rubbed the smooth surface of the golden heart against her cheek. *Ouch!* She jerked the piece from her face and examined it. The ring connecting the heart to the chain appeared jagged, as if ripped off violently. Had someone yanked the locket from Joanna's neck? Kate wondered. Certainly it hadn't fallen off accidentally. She doubted anyone would remove such a precious piece of jewelry so carelessly.

Shaking her head, Kate put the locket back into the drawer. Had there been foul play involved? Or had Joanna merely disappeared or . . . *Stop it! I mustn't think on those lines!*

Kate blew out the lamp and left the room. Determinedly she headed toward the staircase.

I won't think about what people are saying about Joshua Redfield. I'll concentrate on the things Margo had pointed out about him. Think positive, she told herself as she walked down the stairs. To bolster her courage, Kate had put on the dress Jane Kessler had given her. The delicate skirt gently whispered her progress down the steps.

Anna sat on the bottom step, with head in her hands, waiting. She jumped up at the sound of Kate's descent. "I'm waiting to take you to dinner," she explained anxiously. "Do you like it here?"

Kate laughed lightly. "But Anna, I've only just come. So far it is extremely pleasant." She looked about the deserted downstairs. "Your home is breathtaking."

"Breathtaking? What does that mean?" she asked, grabbing her teacher's hand.

"It means so lovely it sort of takes your breath away."

"Like a surprise?" she asked, skipping beside Kate.

"Yes, exactly."

"Josh said I could sit next to you. Aren't you glad?"

"It makes me very happy," Kate said as they entered the formal dining room.

Again Kate lost her breath. The table was clothed in green, with silver candle holders and tableware. Flowers decorated the center, arranged in a large basket. To the right stood another elegant silver candelabrum, upon a buffet that displayed colorful spreads of various foods.

By the window Josh Redfield stood, talking to his father.

Both were dressed formally and would have taken her breath away if the dining room scene hadn't already done it. Kate was especially taken aback by Josh's new look. His beard and mustache no longer grew thick and wild but had been trimmed and groomed carefully.

Josh's eyes seemed unable to leave her, but he hardly spoke a word beyond his curt "Good evening." It was left to Arthur Redfield to say, "My, what a vision you are, Miss Hunter. I hardly expected such stylishness in Kansas."

She smiled only slightly; unsure whether his words were a compliment or criticism, Kate turned toward the table. Which of the ten or more chairs was meant for her? Only the four place settings at the far end, with one prominently placed at the table's head, gave her a clue.

"Sit here!" Anna cried, patting the seat of a gold brocade chair with carved light-colored-wood legs.

"Let's eat," Arthur barked, taking the seat across from Anna, who sat beside her father, at the table head.

Kate silently slid into the chair beside Anna. Never in her whole twenty-one years had she felt more uncomfortable, despite her fine dress. The most formal dinner she'd ever attended had been supper at her minister's parsonage, when her mother was in childbirth with Benji. She trembled within, remembering how she'd spilled her water glass and had run from the room in tears. Of course Mrs. Lewis had run after her and assured her that no one minded. Would anyone mind if she spilled something here? Surely they would. How could she manage to eat under these conditions? She yearned to be back at the kitchen table on their farm or even back at Margo's. She didn't fit in here.

While dishes were passed, she spooned a little of each onto her plate and wondered how she had felt herself more suitable for Geoffrey than Lydia Spencer. Lydia probably came from a more socially acceptable family than she did. Dressing with more taste and a good education weren't enough, she'd realized the moment she'd sat down at this elaborate table. Would the Redfields notice, from her manners, that she wasn't familiar with this type of dining?

After Josh said grace, Kate put her first forkful to her mouth, chewed automatically, without tasting, and swallowed painfully. No one spoke! She wished this meal over quickly.

To Kate's relief Anna broke some of the tension at the table. "We don't always eat like this," she whispered to Kate. "It's because of my grandfather." Anna smiled and said knowingly, "He's used to eating like this in London."

Kate cast a quick look at Arthur, who frowned at his granddaughter. "Did you say something, miss? If so, say it loud enough for all of us to hear."

Feeling responsible for Anna's scolding, Kate cleared her throat and said feebly, "She was telling me you're from London."

The old man smiled proudly. "Born within the sound of the bells, I am."

"I've always wanted to visit England. It's such a fascinating country," Kate said. She noticed that conversing made the meal seem less tense.

"London is stuffy," remarked Joshua. "This country is much more to my liking."

"Humph!" sneered Arthur. "Primitive, I call it."

"Father, it's called country living!"

"*Country!* If that's all you wanted, you could have moved down by Plymouth or Penzance. You didn't have to move across the ocean to live in the country!" Arthur nearly shouted.

"My dear father," Josh said in a humoring tone. "You

know nothing back in England can compare with this. Did you see the richness of the soil? The vastness of the plains? There is only one place I'd trade this for, and that's California. I've heard—"

"That's even farther west!" Arthur sputtered. Picking up his fork, he waved it at Joshua. "You and Joanna just wanted to get away from me. Didn't you?"

I was right, thought Kate. She hardly blamed Joshua, for she could see that once Arthur had an idea, he held to it as firmly as a wolf grasped its prey.

Joshua frowned, and his voice hardened ruthlessly, "This is not the place to discuss that subject."

"I've been here a week, and you haven't shown me a place to discuss it yet!" Arthur spat. "How long do you think I'm planning on staying in this God-forsaken place?"

"We'll discuss this later—" Joshua's voice held warning.

"When?" Arthur pressed. "And where is Joanna? No one has given me a satisfying answer on that subject. Just where is she?"

Embarrassed, Joshua Redfield glanced at Kate and Anna. "You'll have to excuse my father; he's always been high-strung." To Arthur he ground between clenched teeth, "Later!"

Before Arthur could erupt again, Josh addressed Kate. "Mr. O'Brien stopped by today and informed me that there will be no school for the remainder of the week. He'll let us know Sunday, in church, if it will reopen next week. That depends on how many of the children get sick."

Kate nodded and noted that Josh seemed less hostile with his new "tamed" look. "I see. Well, Anna and I can hold our own school. That will keep us busy."

Joshua's eyes swept over her approvingly. "What a splendid idea! You may use the den. It has a desk and several full bookcases. Also feel free to borrow any book that appeals to you."

Kate thanked him and felt relieved when, a few moments later, he excused himself and his father so they might converse privately in the den. With the men gone, Kate realized how good the food actually tasted.

"Where's Mrs. Simcox?" Kate asked Anna.

"She eats in the kitchen or in her room."

"Why?"

"Josh asked her to eat with us, but she won't. I think she doesn't like eating with my grandfather."

"How do you dine when your grandfather isn't here?"

Anna tilted her head and thought for several moments. "We don't use these." She picked up the silver tableware. "They're just for parties.

"We have the table little, and Mrs. Simcox puts on a white one of these," she fingered the green cloth before her. "The candles go in those." She pointed to some pewter candle holders.

"It's more fun eating with Josh and Mrs. Simcox. We laugh more and don't feel so . . . so—"

"Stuffy?" Kate helped.

Anna giggled. "You know big words. Will I ever be as smart as you?"

Kate smiled knowingly. "It's my job to see that you are!"

On her way through the living room to the stairway, Kate overheard arguing male voices, through the door just beyond the stairway, which she supposed led to the den. She wondered, as she climbed the stairs, what caused such disagreement. Had Josh told Arthur about Joanna's disappearance?

Alone in her room, Kate went to the window to close her drapes. She looked down on the lighted room where Josh and Arthur talked. Arthur, standing by the window, with his hands in his pockets, seemed aggravated. What could Josh be telling him? Kate watched him stare out the window, shaking his head in defeat—or was it confusion or even exasperation?

Closing the drapes, Kate prepared for bed. Before blowing out the lamp, she took the locket from the bedside drawer. Rubbing its smooth side with her fingers, she wondered what it would say, could it talk. Would the heart tell her how it got yanked from its chain?

Kate put her hand inside her skirt pocket and felt for the locket. Fingering the necklace slowly, she watched Anna doing her lesson and wondered how to ask her about it. Would seeing it upset her? She didn't want to hurt Anna for anything. Kate gazed out the window and automatically looked up toward her own bedroom window. This must be where Arthur Redfield had stood last night. She admired the gardens below her window and noticed Arthur sitting on a bench, staring blankly. What had Joshua told him last night to make him appear so old and defeated today?

"I'm finished," Anna said proudly, holding her paper high above her head. "If I have all the answers right, will you take me riding?"

Kate slid into her chair behind the desk. "Do you ride?"

Anna nodded. "My horse is named Lightning. Can you tell how fast he is?"

"Is there a slower horse for me to ride?" Kate asked.

"Sure. My mom's horse, Loco."

"*Loco?*" Kate asked in surprise. "What sort of name is that?"

"He can spin round in circles, so Mom let me name him *Loco.*"

"Have you heard from your mother or had any news about her?" Kate asked cautiously.

Anna seemed to hesitate too long for the brief answer she gave. "Nope."

"Yet you seem so much happier," tested Kate.

"I'm talking to God, like you said to."

Letting out a breath of relief, Kate pulled the locket from her pocket. "Whose is this, Anna?" She held the heart out in the palm of her hand.

Anna looked, and her eyes widened. "Where'd you find that? That's my mama's!"

"I thought it might be. I found it on the floor in the closet of my room."

"That's my mama's room. She must have dropped it. Did you see the pictures inside?"

"Yes. The man is your grandfather, but who is the lovely young woman? Not your mother?"

"No. That's Hannah Redfield, my grandmama, Josh's mama."

"Oh," Kate said softly. "Why would your mother carry their pictures in her locket?"

"Because," explained Anna, "it was Hannah's locket."

Why hadn't Kate thought of that? Of course, the locket had been Hannah's. Josh had probably given it to his wife, and she'd left it as Hannah had kept it. That made sense.

"Whose initials are carved into the metal?" Kate asked.

"Josh had it done for my mama."

"I think, then, you should keep it safe for her," said Kate, holding the golden heart out to Anna.

"I'll take it!" A male voice startled them both.

"Mr. Redfield!" Kate gasped. "I didn't know you were there. You frightened us."

"Josh, you're just like granddad, coming into a room like thunder." Anna giggled.

Without smiling or looking at Anna, Josh walked over and practically snatched the locket from Kate. "I'll keep it safe." He put the heart into his breast pocket and turned to greet Anna. "Are you keeping Miss Hunter busy?"

Anna nodded. "Can I take her riding this afternoon?"

"Riding? What a splendid idea! I may stay home today and ride with you. Would you like that?" Josh asked, kissing her hand.

"Yes! Did you hear that, Miss Hunter?" she squealed. "Josh might come, too! Can she ride Loco?"

"Of course she can," he replied, ruffling the child's hair. Walking toward the door, Josh reminded, "Remember, I said *maybe.*"

Kate smiled smoothly, showing nothing of her annoyance with Joshua's brusqueness or his offer to ride with them. Why had he seemed so uncomfortable that she had Joanna's locket?

11

Kate rummaged through her meager wardrobe. What could she wear riding? She held up her only suitable riding skirt and frowned at the frayed hem and the threadbare seat. Would it hold up or embarrass her by ripping as soon as she mounted her horse? She shrugged and carried the old green suit to the window for closer inspection.

A knock at her door momentarily stunned her. Could that be Anna already? She moved to let her in.

"Why, Ayda, what a pleasant surprise! Come in." She held the door wide.

Over her arm Ayda carried a covered garment. "Anna said you were going riding." She uncovered the outfit and held it out to Kate. "Can you use this riding suit? It's practically new."

Kate smiled quickly, then sobered at the thought of whom it had belonged to. "Joanna?" she asked.

Ayda nodded. "She wouldn't mind, I assure you." She

lifted the cover, showing a pleated dark-blue riding skirt with a matching jacket.

Kate touched the velvety material. "How can you be so sure?"

"Because Joanna and I were close friends. She and you would get along famously." Ayda smiled. "In fact, I think you will one day."

Kate sank down onto her bed. "Then you know she is alive?"

Ayda nodded. "Oh, yes. I'm sure she is."

With a puzzled look, Kate asked, "But how can you be so sure, if no one knows what happened?"

"Trust me" was all Ayda said.

Hadn't Margo told Kate to trust Ayda? Wasn't Margo always right? At least so far? "All right, I'll borrow the riding habit, if you're sure Joanna won't mind."

Ayda hung the riding habit in the closet, then walked to the door and hesitated. "Kate, Margo said you've heard some gossip about the Redfields that has you worried—"

Kate interrupted. "Margo said that?"

Ayda nodded. "People are strange creatures. Whenever they don't know the whole story, they think the worst. I wonder if it's because so many lives lack excitement. Perhaps people with nothing else to do crave the suspense of imagining things about others' lives."

"But, Ayda, you must admit, the circumstances here are somewhat mysterious. If Joanna's disappearance involves no foul play, why aren't the facts being given?"

Ayda smiled patiently. "Because those facts involve personal secrets—things no one else has a right to know. Maybe that's why people invent dreadful stories; they don't like not knowing all the details."

"George Plumb heard Josh tell Phillip Barringer that—"

"Please, Kate!" Ayda held up her hand. "I don't even want to hear it."

"But if you hear it, you'll know—"

"So far everything I know about the Redfields, I admire."

"Can you tell me anything to dispel the rumors I've heard?"

Ayda raised her eyebrows and smiled faintly. "If you let yourself get to know Joshua, you won't need anyone to tell you anything. Find out yourself." She closed the door softly behind her.

Frustrated, Kate threw her old riding suit across the room. *Why won't that woman tell me anything?* Surely Ayda knew enough to ease her mind. Did Joshua get rid of his flirtatious wife? Had Joanna run away with Phillip Barringer? She wished she had never heard those horrid rumors. Ayda was right about gossips. But now that they had sown a seed in Kate's mind, she couldn't kill off the plant it had become.

Kate dressed in Joanna's riding habit and one of her own ruffled white blouses. Then she tied her long hair back tight with a blue ribbon, to keep it from her face while she rode, and headed to the stables.

Just as Kate started to mount Loco, a hand shot out to assist her. Josh! She allowed him to help her and marveled at the ease with which he lifted her atop the horse. Her hand grasped his shoulder for support and his tight, muscular body made her feel secure in his strength.

Anna was already on Lightning, and Josh mounted a beautiful cream-colored horse. "That's Lumberjack!" exclaimed Anna.

Kate laughed within herself. Such simple names for such magnificent animals: *Lightning, Loco,* and *Lumberjack!* The Redfields were as down-to-earth as her family. She recalled

Delilah, their milch cow; Samson, the bull; the old yellow cat, Amber; and Skeeter, her droopy-earred beagle. How could she forget the goat, Jezebel, or the mule they had called Moses? The memories made Kate suddenly homesick.

Before Kate realized it, they were riding quite fast and had reached the schoolhouse. Josh reined in at the back door. When Anna and Kate caught up, Josh asked, "Is there anything you need here?"

Kate shook her head, and Josh urged his horse on toward the main road. The girls began to follow his lead, when suddenly Kate's horse began running in circles, as if chasing his own tail. No matter how she tried to straighten him out, Loco insisted on the circles. Kate's eyes frantically sought Anna, who had waited for her; her silent, horrified face begged the child for help.

"Slap him with the reins!" Anna shouted.

Kate couldn't get them in the right position to use them. Before she knew it, she had lost her grip on Loco and was slipping off the saddle. She tried to jump aside and would have succeeded had her ankle not turned, causing her to land headfirst on the ground. Trying to get to her feet, she cried out from the pain, in the ankle. Loco was still circling, biting crazily at his own tail, and headed right for her prone body. Kate froze in terror. At the same moment she heard Anna scream, a strong arm grabbed her beneath her arms and scooped her up. Still panicky, Kate kicked wildly in midair until she suddenly found herself flung onto the back of Lumberjack and held against the strong chest of Joshua Redfield.

"Are you all right?" he asked anxiously. "Where are you hurt?"

Kate's head swam, and as she fought dizziness Josh's

Dangerous Illusions

arms tightened around her. After taking deep breaths, she finally answered, "I'm fine, but my ankle is throbbing terribly. I think I've sprained it."

"We'll take you back to the house," he said, turning his horse abruptly. "C'mon, Anna, we have to go back; your teacher is hurt."

Kate felt strangely subdued in Joshua's protective arms. She looked at his big, crusty hands on the reins. How gentle they'd felt when they had rescued her. How tender his arms had become when he'd had to steady her. Could this man have caused his wife's disappearance? Somehow Kate doubted that those hands could hurt anyone.

When they returned to the house, Josh carried Kate to the bench overlooking the gardens, knelt on one knee, and moved his thumbs gently yet firmly over her ankle. "H-m-m, doesn't seem to be more than a bad turn." He looked up at her, and one of his gentle brown eyes winked. "Katherine, we won't have to shoot you."

Kate was slightly taken aback. Hardly anyone called her Katherine, except her mother, when she was angry with her. Yet Josh's voice hadn't sounded at all hostile. She rather liked the way he said her name.

"That's a relief," she murmured, half laughing, half crying. "But I doubt I can stand on it, nonetheless."

"You won't have to." He scooped her up into his massive, muscular arms and held her against his hard chest. "I'll carry you upstairs and send Ayda in to help you get into bed."

Ayda scurried into Kate's room, a worried look on her face. "Are you sure it's only a sprain?"

Kate nodded. "Do you think I could eat dinner up here tonight, so I can keep off my feet?" she asked hopefully.

"Certainly. You may have to keep off it for a few days." Ayda examined the ankle and shook her head. "Nasty color. I'll get you ready for bed and bring in some salve."

"This is crazy," Kate murmured as the housekeeper undressed her. "I was practically born riding a horse. How could I have fallen from one?"

"They should have explained how to handle Loco. He's gentle and harmless, but for some reason, whenever flies bother his tail, he goes crazy. Joanna would simply smack his tail with the reins, and that would give him relief. It always worked. I'm surprised they didn't tell you."

"Anna tried to, but it was too late. He was already spinning."

"The only reason they keep that animal is because Joanna liked him. She claimed he was less frisky than most," Ayda explained.

"He was perfect, until he started spinning."

Covering Kate with a crisp sheet, Ayda smiled down on her. "It's almost like having Joanna back. I'm glad you came, Kate."

The next afternoon a voice stirred Kate from gentle napping. "Dr. Redfield, here to check his patient," Josh said, entering through the open door. "Ayda said you've been a perfect convalescent."

"She's been the perfect nurse," Kate replied.

Josh pulled the sheet up from the bottom of the bed and looked at her ankle. "Much better. I'd stay off it another day, just to be sure." He covered up her feet again. "How do you feel otherwise?"

Kate nodded. "Fine. A bit bored is all."

"Bored? How about a game of checkers?" His smile was infectious.

She shrugged. "Sure. I have a few minutes."

Moments later he returned with a box, which he laid upon the empty side of the bed. Pulling up a chair, he asked, "Can you roll onto your side and face this direction?"

Turning, Kate saw he had the game laid out on the sheet. She hadn't played checkers in years. How easily she had beaten Benji and Em, but she'd never won against her father. Josh reminded her of her father, always one jump ahead.

"You won't be able to attend church this week," Josh said, jumping her game piece. "I'll talk to O'Brien and give you his decision on the school."

"Have you heard if anyone else has come down with measles?"

"Only one more."

"Who?"

"One of the Balcombs. The girl, I think."

"Lucy?"

"I guess."

Kate smiled as she finally captured one of his men. "I suppose the boys will get them now."

"Probably. But Buzz said they were keeping the others away from the sick one. Sometimes that works."

As Kate watched him plan his strategy she wished he would turn the conversation to Joanna. She wanted the mystery solved, so she could decide if she liked this man, Joshua Redfield, or despised him.

But moments later, Ayda came to the door and announced that Kate had visitors. She twisted around to see Geoffrey and Lydia walking into her room.

Geoffrey nodded toward Josh. "Lydia and I came to see

our clumsy equestrian. We certainly thought you knew how to ride by now!" Geoffrey teased.

Lydia shushed him. "He thought all day to come up with something to rile you with. How's the ankle?"

"Much better. They take very good care of me here."

Geoffrey disdainfully glanced at Josh, who was putting the unfinished game back into the box. "Yes, we can see that they are."

"I was bored," Kate explained. "Josh was kind enough to console me with a game of checkers."

"How quaint," Geoffrey said, turning to look out the window.

Lydia smiled at Joshua. "Who won?"

"No one," he said, moving toward the door. "We didn't finish."

"I'm sorry, Josh." Kate wondered why he was leaving. "You don't have to go."

He hurried out, calling over his shoulder, "You won't get off so easily. I'll be back tomorrow with my game—I was ahead you know!"

Kate turned to her guests. "He has been so wonderful; everyone here has been. . . ." Tears filled her eyes. "I can't even think of a word to describe how they've treated me. I can't thank them enough."

"They *should* treat you well," sniffed Geoffrey haughtily. "If it weren't for their inadequate horse, you wouldn't have been hurt."

"You heard the story?" Kate asked, rather offended at his attitude.

"The groom here told Margo," said Geoffrey. "They could have told you how that horse acted."

"You shouldn't have been given such a horse," agreed Lydia.

Kate didn't like the tone of the visit, so she changed the subject. "How are things at the store?"

"Great," remarked Lydia. "I sold everything today!"

"Everything?" Kate asked. "Even the cakes?"

"By four o'clock every baked good except one loaf of bread was gone. Margo decided we'd use it ourselves for supper."

"But then the Mullins family didn't get anything!" Kate said.

"No, but I hear their babies, Emmet and Eleanor, are sick with measles. Just when Randy was getting well, too. Didn't Ayda mention it?"

"No. I pray they'll be well soon."

"Actually," said Lydia, "the doctor's most concerned with Clara. She's taken quite ill, and Harley has all he can do to care for them all."

"Don't be surprised," added Geoffrey, "if Ayda has to leave here to take care of them."

"But she can't!" exclaimed Kate. "I can't stay in a home with two men and a small girl. If she leaves, where will I go?"

12

*T*rue to his word, the next afternoon, after he returned from the lumberyard, Josh came into Kate's room,
carrying the checkers game.

The first thing he did was look at her ankle. "It's mending
nicely. Look, no more black and purple, but a soft yellow!"
He winked.

"To match my bed jacket." Kate enjoyed the warm and
enchanting tone of Josh's humor.

"Did you think you'd get out of playing checkers?" he
asked, hands on his hips.

"No," she replied. "I knew you'd be back."

"And just how did you know that?"

"I can tell a man of his word."

"If more people thought that of me, I'd lose half of my
problems."

Kate saw an opportunity to fish into his personal life.
"What problems could you possibly have?"

"Ha!" He threw back his head and let out the peal of

laughter. *"What problem don't I have?* would be a more apt question."

"By the looks of this house, you have no financial worries. Your daughter is bright, beautiful, and extremely healthy. Your housekeeper is loyal and hard working. . . . Need I go on?" she asked.

His eyes sparkled. "Yes, I thank God daily for my blessings. But don't judge a man's wealth by the size of his house; I merely got a good price on the lumber. While I'm not exactly rich, my business has been successful, thanks to the people of Victoria."

"Then what could possibly trouble you?" she asked hopefully.

"Most of my problems are not actually mine, but those of others. I became enmeshed in them because I care."

Kate bit her lip. Dare she ask directly about Joanna or the gossip? No, she didn't know Josh well enough to pry into his life. She waited, hoping he'd offer something.

Josh watched her for several seconds before clapping his hands together. "Are you ready to get beaten at checkers?"

They made several moves on the checkerboard without speaking. Finally Josh opened with: "I hope we can finish before your friend comes to visit." His mouth twisted into a cynical smile.

"My *friend?*" Kate had detected a note of censure in his tone.

"I hope you don't mind if I make an observation about yesterday." He continued without waiting for her to comment, "When your friend walked into the room, your eyes lit up like two flaming candles. Yet you have only known each other a short time. Hardly long enough to form such a close relationship."

"What?" To her annoyance, Kate found herself starting

to blush. "I've known Geoffrey since I came here and am extremely fond of him. If my eyes lit up—which I doubt they did—it would have been from surprise. I never expected to see him here!"

"Amazing," he answered, his eyes sparkling mischievously from under bushy eyebrows. "I was referring to your friendship with Lydia, not Geoffrey."

"You baited me!" she cried, throwing her game piece down. "The game is over!" She turned over in bed, leaving him looking at her back. "Please close the door on your way out."

"Aha," he said impishly. "I think you just don't want to play. Some people can't stand to lose."

Kate turned and glared at him. "What do you mean by that?"

"I mean . . . ," he stood up and collected his game, "there are people who are afraid to play games because they're afraid of losing. Then there are those who refuse to play because they fear they might win."

"Is that supposed to mean something?" She sat up straight and glared at him.

"As a matter of fact, it does." He glared back.

"You don't make sense!"

"You're afraid of losing, and I'm afraid of winning. Therefore we'll never finish the game, will we?"

She digested this for several moments before asking in a childlike voice, "Are you still talking about checkers?"

He walked to the door. "Anyone can see you're in love or at least infatuated with Geoffrey Grandville. Do you really want him? Then let him know how you feel. Lydia isn't as attractive or smart as you—or are you afraid? Afraid of losing?"

Stunned into speechlessness, Kate felt her mouth drop.

How had he seen so much? Should she admit to her feelings? She flipped over, showing him her back again, and said over her shoulder, "You have a vivid imagination. I don't know what you are talking about. Lydia and Geoffrey are my friends. How dare you even say such a thing?"

He turned to leave.

"Wait a minute, don't you go yet!"

Josh froze and looked back at her with questions in his eyes.

"Come back here!"

He retraced his steps and faced her, amusement apparent in his eyes. Their lively twinkle incensed Kate. *How dare he?*

"You have some nerve accusing me of loving my friend's betrothed! We've never done anything improper. What about your own life? Just where is Joanna? Why do people say there was foul play involved with her disappearance? Is she even alive?" Kate demanded furiously.

Josh's brown eyes clouded in anger; his eyebrows twitched, and his temples throbbed. Kate knew the man was close to exploding. *Have I pushed him too far? Why couldn't I have held my temper in check?*

Yet Josh remained silent, seeming to fight within himself to gain control. Finally he turned toward the door, his tone civil, despite his anger. "If you're finished, I'll leave."

"What are you afraid of, Josh Redfield? Have you no answers?" Kate accused him gently, for she now feared arousing his temper again. "Have you nothing to say?" She asked calmly, her eyes blazing.

His voice was cold when he answered, "To clear my name, I'd have to tell secrets that aren't mine to divulge. I can't do that! People can think whatever they want. I know the truth, and I have nothing to feel guilty about."

"Surely you can tell a child if her mother is alive or dead!" Kate countered icily. "What about her suffering?"

Quick anger arose in his eyes. "That's enough! Leave Anna out of this!" His face reddened, and Kate knew she'd pushed too far, yet she was too fired up to back down now.

"People think you *murdered* your wife! Anna has already been hurt by hearing that! She misses her mother. How can you protect someone's secret at the cost of your own child's welfare?"

His anger simmered into frustration. "But you don't understand! I'm trying to solve those problems. I need time!"

"You'll never erase the hurt all this has caused Anna." Her anger abated into annoyance.

Josh's sensitive eyes filled. "How can I help Anna now?"

Kate's heart wrenched at the pain in his face. "Can you give her her mother back?"

Josh straightened and partly composed himself. "At what price, Katherine? At what price?" The once tall, proud man walked out of the room, old, slumped, and emotionally drained.

Elated that she'd found Josh did have a soft spot— Anna—Kate completely forgot her anger at his remarks about Geoffrey. Though Josh would do almost anything for this little girl, it seemed, something held him back. Loyalty? To whom? What *was* he hiding?

Kate searched all Josh's words. Before, when she'd asked about Joanna, she hadn't hit any sore spots. What had he said? Kate could only remember his answer, "I have no wife." Did that mean she was dead? Kate punched her pillow in frustration.

Josh had been terribly upset the day he snatched the locket from her hand. What had made him react that way?

And if the locket had belonged to his mother, why did it have *Joanna's* initials on it?

So many things didn't add up. Ayda seemed so certain Joanna remained alive. How could Kate reconcile that with the conversation George Plumb had overheard between Josh and the mysterious Phillip Barringer? Her mind teemed with doubts.

Josh's reaction to Kate's questions had somehow changed things. Perhaps the pain in his eyes had aroused her sympathy. Had she sensed the innate honesty and truthfulness of this man?

He'd been the only one—besides Margo—to pick up on her feelings for Geoffrey. She wondered if she'd been so obvious.

Kate punched her pillow again, wondering what Josh had meant when he'd said that she was afraid of losing and he afraid of winning.

Yes, she admitted, she *was* afraid to openly make her feelings known to Geoffrey. *But what could Josh be afraid of winning? If rumor has the correct story he has already lost. Hasn't Phillip Barringer made off with his wife?*

After dinner, Kate sat in the rocking chair in front of her curving windows, reading a book. Her door stood open, for she hoped Josh would come by to apologize. Footsteps stopped outside her door, and she looked up. Margo stood, hands on hips, surveying Kate.

"You certainly have made a life for yourself!" she smiled mischievously. "And you were afraid to come here! *I* should have it this good!"

"Margo! How great to see you! Come in and sit down."

"I'm a bearer of sad news, I'm afraid." Margo took a seat in the gold brocade chair by the closet. Folding her hands neatly in her lap, she faced Kate. "The measles are spreading."

"No." Kate shook her head. "That means the school stays closed, right?"

"I'm afraid so. But that isn't the worst. Have you ever had measles?"

Kate shook her head.

"These are the worst cases Doc Oliver has seen in years. He claims you couldn't place a pin between the spots on Randy Mullins—they were that close together.

"We only have one doctor here, and he's completely worn out treating these children. Another one, from Dodge City, is coming to help." Margo played nervously with her hands.

"That isn't the worst news, is it?" Kate asked, adding quickly, "How are the twins?"

"Fine, so far. Thank the Lord."

"What else is wrong, then?"

"It's Clara Mullins, she's extremely unwell."

"Measles?"

"They don't think so, but. . . ." She shrugged.

"What then?"

"Her pregnancy. Doc thinks the baby is dead. Two of her other children are sick with measles; now she's ready to go into labor any time and have a stillborn child." Tears glittered in Margo's eyes.

"Is there anything we can do?" Kate asked.

"Yes. Ayda has been called to be with her daughter. She'll stay with her until—"

"I can understand that," Kate said thoughtfully. "Geoffrey mentioned yesterday that this might happen. But where should *I* go now?"

Margo shook her head sadly. "Not only are none of the

children's homes safe for you, I'm worried about Lydia."

"Lydia?" Kate frowned. "Why?"

"She's never had measles either. I thought perhaps she could come here with you. She would be a proper chaperon—you wouldn't have to share your room, because Josh said—"

"You talked to Josh about this already?"

"Why, yes. We visited downstairs before I came up. He said he has another room—not as large as this, but nice—that she could use."

"Then I can stay?" Kate asked.

"It's the perfect solution."

"Can we do anything for Clara Mullins and her family?"

"Because Ayda is with her daughter and can't be here, Josh needs a housekeeper, especially with extra guests. I assured him you and Lydia would take over most of Ayda's duties."

"Margo! *Me*? A house this size?"

"Certainly you helped your mother, back on the farm?"

"Sure, but. . . . Ayda did everything so efficiently."

"You don't have to be as perfect as Ayda, just help out. Lydia is the one I'm concerned about."

"Why?" Kate asked, feeling somewhat annoyed with the sympathy this girl was managing to get from Margo.

"She isn't exactly cut out for domesticity. I've tried everything. She's excellent in the store. But ask her to boil water, and she boils the pot dry, and it burns."

"She really did *that*?"

Margo held up her right hand. "Honest."

"Does Geoffrey know?" Kate asked.

"I haven't had the courage to tell him. He thinks I'm the ideal housewife and mother, and if I teach Lydia, then she'll be just like me."

Kate frowned. "You have to tell him. He has a right to know."

Margo fidgeted in her chair. "Yes, I know . . . but. . . ."

"But what? Tell him," Kate insisted. "I told you she isn't right for him." Though his actions toward Josh had slightly disillusioned her, still Kate clung to this chance for love.

Margo shook her head sadly. "I'll tell him. I sort of hoped, coming here, that you might help. . . . You know, sort of show her. . . ." Margo looked at Kate hopefully. "Will you?"

"Me! Why me?"

"Because she's so fond of you, and her mind will be off the store, while she's here. Perhaps she can concentrate on housekeeping more."

"She's never cleaned, either?"

Margo shook her head. "They had a maid."

"Good gracious!" Kate exclaimed. "My teaching is limited, I'm afraid, to schoolwork. I don't know—"

"Well, Kate," Margo stood, "she's coming here tomorrow, so that you can stay. Perhaps you can repay that debt by teaching her something. Whatever you can do to help, I'll appreciate."

When Margo had gone, a conscience-stricken Kate closed her door and slid to her knees, beside the bed, and prayed, "Dear heavenly Father: You know how confused I feel about Geoffrey. How can I give . . .? I mean how can I . . .? Lord, I don't even know how to say it.

"I *like* Lydia, truly I do, but she and Geoffrey don't seem right for each other. Doesn't this prove it? But I don't think it's fair that I should be placed in this situation. If I teach her to be a good wife to Geoffrey, I lose. . . ."

What had she said? The words had slipped out, but once said, she wondered. *Had* Josh been right?

After much thought, she finished her prayer: "Please help me to do what is *right*, Lord. I know You want me to help. Your Word says that we should love our neighbors as ourselves. But that isn't always easy. I need Your help. Show me the way. Thank You, Lord. Amen."

13

*E*arly the next morning, Kate hobbled down to the kitchen for a cup of tea and was reminded that Ayda had gone. There wasn't even a fire started in the old stove. Someone had brought in wood, and a fresh bucket of water sat near the kitchen pump. Kate looked about. Where to begin?

Starting up the oven was easy; she'd done it many times on the farm, and their stove had been smaller and harder to work with. She filled the teapot and placed it on the stove to boil. Opening all the cupboard doors, she planned breakfast. There was oatmeal, fresh bread, and a small basket of apples.

Quickly she began peeling apples. She hadn't made Mom's apple pan cake in years. Scanning the shelf over the stove, she found cinnamon, cloves, and ginger. In large metal canisters she discovered flour and sugar. What about eggs? Where would they be? Back home, the egg basket would have been placed by the back door. She wondered if the Redfields had chickens.

As she mused, Josh came in, wearing a tan jacket and carrying an armload of wood to the stove.

"You've started the fire?" He gave her a look of utter disbelief.

"Certainly," she said with confidence. "Did you think I couldn't do anything but teach school?"

He shrugged and pulled four eggs from his pocket. "Will these do? We only have a few hens. They've been strangely disappearing. Henry, our hired man, says he thinks it's the work of a wolf."

"A—a wolf?" she asked with wide eyes.

He nodded. "Need any help?"

"You can see about Anna. I haven't visited her yet today. Do you suppose she's still sleeping?"

"I'll check." He walked past the stove. "By the way, the oatmeal's boiling!"

"Thanks." She frowned. "I can manage."

He looked from the oatmeal to her. "Yes, I believe you can."

Lovinia Hunter had often made the apple cake, and Kate believed it was her own recipe. She sliced and precooked apples and poured them onto the bottom of a greased square cake pan. She then poured a mixture of flour, water, eggs, baking powder, and spices over the apples. When the cake was baked, she flipped it over so the soft, warm apples topped the cake. Josh ate three pieces of the warm treat.

Anna, who knew where everything was and how things were usually done, helped Kate wash the dishes and clean the kitchen.

Next they began making beds. They had started with

Anna's, when Lydia came in with Margo. Lydia put her arms around Kate. "This will be such fun!" she cried.

Kate agreed. "But there's a good deal of work to be done in a house this size. If we all help, it will be done and we still can have time for ourselves."

"Where should I start? I'm not good at domestic things, but I'm anxious to learn." Lydia helped Kate and Anna smooth the wrinkles from Anna's bedspread.

"Anna, you begin dusting, while Lydia and I finish the beds. C'mon." She nudged Lydia. "Josh's room is next."

"He isn't in there, is he?"

"No. He left for the lumberyard. Probably won't be back until dinner." Kate pointed Lydia in the right direction.

Margo exited quickly, calling over her shoulder, "I'm leaving before I get assigned a job!"

Joshua Redfield's room was immaculate. He hadn't made his bed, but he had smoothed it out. The man obviously slept lightly, for his bed was simple to make.

His dresser tops were clear, except for a wooden jewelry box and a few grooming articles. He'd emptied and cleaned his washbowl and other bed pots.

"Where to next?" asked Lydia.

"My room. Go on ahead, I'll scoop up his dirty laundry and put it with ours." On her way to the closet, Kate noticed the top on Josh's jewelry box was askew. She lifted it to peek inside before straightening it. A large-stoned ring blinked at her. She picked it up. A ruby perhaps? She slipped it on each finger until she found one that it fit: her thumb. *He sure has big fingers*, she thought. Replacing the ruby carefully, she spied another ring beneath it, a plain gold band. The ring was quite worn and fit perfectly on Kate's third finger. Certainly not his. Joanna's? Was this the one they found in pocket, after Joanna disappeared? She removed the ring and took it to the window, for better light. Peering inside, she could see a faint initial or date, but it was worn too badly to decipher. She replaced the ring and closed the box, scolding herself for snooping. If she hadn't sneaked, her doubts about Josh wouldn't have returned.

Kate entered her own room and burst into peals of laughter, until her eyes began to water. Lydia stared at her, then glanced around the room for the object of her hysteria. The innocence of her naive look sent Kate into harder pangs of glee.

"Kate! What is wrong?" Lydia asked. "Have you gone crazy?"

Unable to stop laughing, Kate held her sore abdomen. She pointed at the bed.

"I made the bed," Lydia replied.

When Kate continued to point, Lydia looked more puzzled. "Kate, if you don't stop at once, I'll scream. What is wrong?"

Kate plopped into her rocking chair and composed herself. My, but her stomach hurt! Blowing her nose and drying her eyes, she sighed. "Oh Lydia! Did you even look at the bed, after you made it?"

The innocent-faced Lydia came around and examined her work. "Oh dear, whatever is that thing hanging down?"

"My dressing gown! You made my dressing gown into the bed. The arm and belt are hanging on the floor."

Immediately Lydia began unmaking the bed. "I didn't even see it, honest! I'm so sorry!"

"Actually, I needed a good laugh," Kate said.

Lydia stopped remaking the bed and dropped on her knees before the rocker. "I need your help terribly, Kate.

I'm a complete failure at everything Geoffrey wants me to learn. Do you think he's changed his mind about marrying me?"

"Why do you say that?" Kate asked.

"He seems disappointed. And sometimes he looks at me funny."

Kate laughed. "How? What do you mean, *funny?*"

"It's hard to explain, but almost critically. Could it be that he doesn't like the way I dress or do my hair? He often hints at ways I could look better."

"Hints? Such as. . . ," Kate prodded.

"Sometimes I get so jealous of you! Then I remember that you're my best friend and—"

"Me? Why *me?*" Kate asked.

"Because sometimes Geoffrey makes remarks like: 'Why don't you try wearing your hair like Kate's?' Or, 'Kate really knows how to dress.' Things like that."

Excitement stirred in Kate until she looked at Lydia's forlorn face.

"Will you help me with my appearance? I'd like to be more like you."

Conflicting emotions swept through Kate. Warmth at Geoffrey's kind words welled up, followed by sympathy for Lydia, who loved this man so much she'd sacrificed her whole way of life for him.

Guilt at her own selfish attitude hit Kate. When had *she* ever thought of giving up something for Geoffrey? No, instead her mind had focused on all the benefits his life-style would bring her. She'd expected a storybook hero, who would sweep her off into a world of chivalry and ease—so unlike anything in Kansas!

I never thought of what would please him—or God, Kate

thought sorrowfully. *Though I never meant to lose sight of what was right, I let it slip out of my life.*

Looking back at the one time she had seen Geoffrey since she'd moved in with the Redfields, Kate began to understand the depth of his emotion for Lydia. *Why, he probably only came because Lydia wanted to call*, she realized. *He'd never have stopped by on his own.*

Kate tried to think charitably about the Englishman, but she had a hard time forgiving him for his haughtiness toward Josh Redfield. *Josh was so kind to me, entertaining me when I could hardly leave my bed. Yet Geoffrey looked at him as if he were a worm!* Suddenly the idea that Geoffrey might show interest in her no longer filled Kate with elation.

Turning her thoughts back to the engaged couple, Kate decided she could never have done as Josh had suggested and told Geoffrey of her interest: That would have broken her best friend's heart. *If Lydia loves him enough to learn to live well in this land*, Kate decided, *I can love her enough to help her become what Geoffrey needs.* As long as they cared so selflessly for each other, the couple had the main ingredient that would make each happy, no matter what their differences. Kate could simply alter and rearrange Lydia's skills to fit Geoffrey's ideal.

"Of course I'll help you. We're best friends, are we not?" For the first time Kate knew she really meant those words. "When I get finished with you, Geoffrey will think he died and went to heaven!"

"Oh, thank you!" Lydia cried.

"C'mon, girl, we have plenty of work ahead of us. We're going to check our stores, make out a shopping list, and start planning our dinner. Follow me, watch everything I do, and take mental notes. The most important part of running a smooth household is orderliness. Everything must be in its place, and the kitchen should be well stocked. Cleanliness *is* next to godliness."

Kate stopped short in the doorway and turned around to face Lydia. "Your mother didn't teach you anything? Not even about clothes and what matches and what doesn't?"

"My mother died when I was born," she replied. "My father reared me."

"I'm sorry," Kate whispered.

"Dad did the best he could. We never lacked money, but Dad wasn't domestic either. He became a sort of work horse and spent almost all his time at the bank or at meetings."

"Don't worry." Kate put her arms around Lydia and experienced love for her as she'd never felt before. "You're in good hands now!"

When Josh returned, Kate handed him the shopping list. Giving her a strange look she couldn't define, he put it into his pocket. "I'll bring your order home Monday," he said and continued walking.

"Oh, by the way," she called, causing him to stop and turn around. "There are a few items on the list that are personal. I'll pay you for them."

He nodded and turned toward his room, but he seemed to change his mind. He spun around. "Kate! May I have a word with you?"

"Sure." She met him halfway between her room and his.

"I'm sorry," he said simply. "I said some things I had no right to say. I have no excuse, but I'm sorry."

After seeing the sincerity in his eyes, Kate responded, "I'm sorry, too. Isn't it strange how our tongues will fight the battles for our bruised hearts?"

*   *   *

Kate put Lydia to work in the kitchen, chopping vegetables, kneading bread, washing potware, and assisting with all the cooking. Kate was pleased with most of her work, though she had to explain everything carefully. Lydia seemed anxious to learn, and Kate thought she deserved an A for effort, though she'd get only a C for her performance.

Because she alone knew how it should be done, Anna set the dining room table. Lydia added a few touches picked up from social functions in New York: She folded one linen napkin fancily, and the little girl eagerly imitated it for every place setting.

Despite the fact that Kate lacked Ayda's expertise, the dinner of stew and biscuits was a success: Everyone raved about the food.

But as she ran into the kitchen for the third time, leaving behind her unfinished meal, Kate wondered, *How does Ayda get everything on the table at the same time?*

Seeing her distress, Josh simply comforted her, "I prefer my biscuits last; I can clean my plate with them."

Surprisingly, Arthur Redfield gave her the best compliment. "This stew reminds me of Hannah and our house in Coventry. She did all her own cooking, before the accident. An excellent job she did, too!"

"Accident?" asked Kate. "Is that how she died?"

"No, no, she lived ten years after that but was never quite the same. I had to hire a housekeeper. Hannah looked after the children herself, though," Arthur added proudly.

Kate suddenly wanted to know more about this family. "What type of accident?"

"Her carriage was hit broadside by a drunken, no-good rake named—"

"Father, calm down! That was almost twenty-five years ago. It's over with. Why can't you forgive and forget?"

"Never!" he spat. "I'll *never* forget, so how can I forgive?"

Kate jumped up to get dessert. When she returned, several moments later, with hot bread pudding, the conversation had switched to politics. As the men ranted and disagreed on the running of the two nations, the girls ate quietly.

Anna worried about how soon the school would open, so she could be the fortunate one to accompany the teacher. Lydia thought about impressing Geoffrey with all her new domestic skills. Kate wondered about Hannah Redfield and her accident. Dare she ask questions? The main topic at the table generally was introduced by the men. Women shared but rarely controlled table conversation. It was poor etiquette. Silently Kate sat, suffering from her own curiosity.

The measles outbreak had caused church services to be canceled. After dinner Josh informed them all that a short Bible reading would take place at nine the next morning, in the den.

The girls dragged themselves to their rooms early, and Kate fell asleep as soon as her head touched the pillow. Yet on Sunday she rose with the sun, started a fire in the stove, and made preparations for breakfast.

Josh and Lydia joined Kate and helped her make hotcakes. Everyone, except Arthur, assisted in meal preparation and cleanup.

After breakfast Arthur begged off from the Bible reading, explaining he had a headache, so Josh read two chapters of Psalms to the girls. Following prayer, Josh thanked them for their help and commended their work they've done so far.

"However," he added, "this is the sabbath, our day of

rest. Although it isn't always possible to remain completely at leisure, we can all help each other on Sunday, to make everyone's duties minimal. Do as little as possible today. I'll be here to help with meals, but we'll keep them simple.

"Any of that delicious stew left over?" he asked Kate.

When she nodded, he asked, "Enough for another meal?" At her second nod, he said, "Good. That will be dinner. For lunch we'll finish off Ayda's chicken soup. Everyone is responsible for his own bedroom on Sunday, so you ladies can do whatever you enjoy."

Before leaving them, he added, "If I may make a few suggestions, Anna has every type of needlework you can imagine, from her mother. The den is filled with books. Just remember, our evening Bible reading is immediately after dinner cleanup."

They thanked him. When he'd gone, all three girls looked at one another and shrugged. "What do you want to do?" they all spoke at once. They laughed, and Kate took control of the situation. "Anna, could you teach Lydia some needlework? She'd love to learn." Kate prodded the other woman with her elbow, "Wouldn't you, Lydia?"

"What?" She looked about, puzzled. "Oh, yes, I'd love to learn how to make things for the house. What can you teach me?" she asked Anna.

"I can show you how to embroider, crochet, or knit," boasted Anna. "Which do you want to learn first?"

Lydia looked to Kate for help.

"Crocheting," Kate stated with assurance. "You can make doilies for your home and different types of fancy trim for your clothes. When your first lesson is finished, we'll do something different with your hair."

Lydia beamed. "All right. But what will you be doing?"

"I've been wanting to look over the books in the den. If I find something, I'll be in my room, reading."

Running her fingers along the spines of the numerous volumes in the bookcase, Kate pulled one out, looked at it closely, shoved it back into its place, and browsed more. A shadow fell on her. She spun around.

"Mr. Redfield! Sir, you frightened me! I didn't hear you enter."

"That's because I didn't. I was in the corner when you came in. Are you bored, too?" he asked, scanning the books.

"Not bored, no. Merely anxious to relax and enjoy the day. Housekeeping is hard work. I appreciate our day of rest."

"You remind me so much of Hannah." He sighed.

Glad the subject was once again where she could learn about the Redfields, Kate jumped at the opportunity to chat. So many questions flooded her mind: *How many children did you have besides Joshua? How badly was Hannah hurt in the accident? Was anyone else hurt? How did Hannah die?* But before she could voice one Josh burst into the den, his eyes flashing with impatience.

14

"*F*ather, did you forget we had an appointment?" Joshua demanded from the doorway, frowning.

"*Appointment?*" he asked.

"Father, how could you forget something this important?"

The old man shook his head. "I didn't really forget about it." He took out his pocket watch. "I merely forgot the time, is all."

Josh threw him an impatient glare. "Well! Let's get going! The horses are ready."

Arthur's voice faded as he walked down the hall to the front door, "You're not giving me that Loco horse to ride, are you?"

Kate sighed. She'd almost had the opportunity to find out more about the Redfields. As she scanned the rows of books, she made a mental note to approach Arthur alone for a chat. She pulled out a thin book from the shelf and read: *Pride and Prejudice*, by Jane Austen. Perfect for an afternoon's reading. Tucking it under her arm, she hurried up the stairs to enjoy it while everything was quiet.

Kate opened her door and made for the rocking chair. A strange smell stopped her short. She sniffed. Lavender! She didn't have any scent like that. Where had the smell come from? She looked about but found nothing. Shrugging, she curled up in the chair and enjoyed the romantic tale of the Bennet sisters.

As soon as she started reading about the haughty Mr. Darcy, Kate began to compare him to Geoffrey. Surely Geoffrey was more warmhearted than the fictional character, but Kate began to understand a bit more why the earl's son acted as he did. Perhaps the influences of his native land had shown in the response he and the other Victorians had to hard work and their attitudes toward others. It would be hard to break from a life-style of many years.

I know Geoffrey wants to make this settlement last, Kate thought. *But can he turn his back on a pleasure-loving past?* She hoped so, for Lydia's sake.

Despite the charms of her romantic tale, Kate fell asleep and was only awakened by Lydia's gentle shaking. "Kate! Wake up!"

"Oh-h-h!" Kate stretched. "What is it, Lydia?" She closed her eyes, ready to fall back asleep.

"You promised to do something new to my hair. Josh said he'd be ready to help prepare dinner in an hour, so I thought, if we hurried, we'd still have time."

"All right, I did promise." Kate stood and yawned. "You'll have to read this after I'm finished. It's very amusing." She tossed the book onto the bed. "Come, let's begin. Sit here by the dressing table."

Kate brushed Lydia's hair until it almost shone. While she worked Kate asked, "How was your sewing lesson?"

"Wonderful," replied Lydia. "Except I hate counting all those little loops. Anna's a great little teacher, but soon lost patience with me, I'm afraid. She seemed relieved when we were interrupted."

"Interrupted? How?" Kate asked.

"A lady knocked at Anna's bedroom door and asked to speak with her for a few moments. Anna didn't waste any time leaving me to count loops and drop stitches."

"Was she gone long?"

Lydia shrugged. "Longer than I'd thought she'd be. Whoever the woman was, I didn't think she'd keep Anna for over a half hour. By the time she came back, I'd completely lost control of my sample square. At the end of ten rows, instead of eighteen stitches, I only had twelve left. My sample square looked like a triangle!"

Kate laughed with Lydia, then sobered. "What did this lady look like?" Kate couldn't imagine who'd visit Anna.

"She only stuck her head in the door for a second." Lydia thought for a moment. "She was young and pretty, with blond hair and blue eyes." Lydia shrugged. "There was nothing else about her to recall . . . except—"

"Except, what?" prodded Kate.

"Her perfume or sachet. She left a distinct aroma behind. I'm trying to think of what that smell was. Not violets. . . ."

"Lavender?"

"Lavender! That's it! I once had lavender powder, so I'm

sure that's it." Lydia looked anxious. "Does that tell you who the visitor is?"

Kate shook her head. "I'm afraid not. All it tells me is that the same woman was here in my room before I came up to read."

"Your room smelled of lavender?"

Kate nodded. "But I don't have any such scent."

"Who would be in your room? Surely not either of the men. Ayda's not here. Margo?"

Kate shook her head. "Maybe it was Joanna Redfield?" Lydia's eyes widened. "Let's go visit Anna."

Both women rushed down the hall and skidded to a stop before Anna's door. Lydia knocked lightly, and Kate called out, "Anna? Are you in there?"

There was no answer. They sighed with disappointment. "She must have gone downstairs already." Kate frowned. "Let's go down. Maybe she's alone, and we can talk to her."

They bounded down the stairs, to find Anna playing checkers with her grandfather. Kate and Lydia walked by, greeting them casually.

"Are you going to start dinner now?" Anna asked, looking up from her gameboard.

"Yes, but you finish. It's early yet," Kate told her. Smiling at Arthur, she asked sweetly, "How was your appointment? Were you on time?"

"Drat! What a waste of time that was! Our party never showed! A blasted wild goose chase it was, and if you think I'm prone to a tantrum, you should've seen my son! He's usually the calm, sensible one. Why, I had to smooth *his* feathers for a change."

"Perhaps the person who never showed up had the same problem remembering the appointment that you did!" Kate laughed. "So don't be so hard on him. To err is human—"

". . . To forgive, divine. I know that one! The saying is certainly true of this person. No one errs more than—"

"Father," Josh interrupted for the second time that day. "We're going to prepare a quick dinner then, immediately after, hold our evening devotions. Will you be joining us?"

The old man fidgeted. "After dinner? You mean right after? I—I don't know. . . . I think I have something—" He pulled at his collar nervously.

"Nonsense! You can join us!" Josh stated. "Are you gals ready to work small miracles in the kitchen?" Josh called over his shoulder.

After dinner cleanup they settled in the den and read from the Bible. Kate enjoyed the selection, but Arthur fell asleep, and Anna seemed unusually nervous.

They closed in prayer, led by Josh, and Kate marveled at his eloquence in talking to God. While his prayer was "off the cuff," he had chosen his words perfectly. As he prayed Kate shivered, wondering, *How could a man who prays so beautifully be capable of harming anyone?* She decided to find Anna's mother and bring her back herself, if she had to. Silently Kate prayed for this purpose, as well as the concerns brought before God by Josh.

As the girls climbed the stairs Kate playfully tugged on one of Anna's blond pigtails. "Want to come to my room for a story or something, after you get ready for bed?"

Anna smiled. "Sure! It won't take me long!" She rushed to her room, waving to Lydia.

"You want to talk to her alone, right?" Lydia winked.

Kate nodded. "I think it's best. Good night. And don't

forget, I'm waking you up at the crack of dawn to help start the fire for breakfast!"

"Knock lightly. If I don't answer, feel free to go on without me!" Lydia laughed, ducking into her room and closing the door.

Kate donned her blue flannel nightgown, for the wind howled fiercely at the windows. *We might get a first frost tonight,* she thought. She brushed her hair vigorously until she heard Anna's familiar knock at her door.

Anna jumped excitedly onto Kate's bed and covered her bare feet with her nightgown. "What story will you tell?"

"I think," began Kate, sitting cross-legged beside her, "that it's *you* who'll be telling *me* the story tonight."

Confused, Anna tilted her head at Kate. "But I don't know any story good enough to tell."

"That's *well* enough, and it isn't a book story I want to hear, but a real-life story."

Anna gave Kate another puzzled look.

"Who was the lady visitor Lydia said you had today?"

Kate saw the color fade from Anna's face. "L-lady?"

"Yes. You had a lady visitor. Who was it?"

"What if she made me promise not to tell?" Anna asked.

"Then I shall tell your father about it. He should know about visitors who talk privately with his daughter."

"No!" cried Anna. "Don't tell Josh!"

Kate sighed. "Anna, was the visitor your mama?"

Anna nodded, her eyes full of tears.

"Does she visit you often?"

"Only two times. She came just after you told me to pray."

"Anna, what is happening? How can I help, if I don't know the whole story?"

"You would help?" she asked hopefully.

"Of course I would."

"We could trust you not to tell Josh or my grandfather?"

"Certainly. We women have to stick together, don't we?" Kate pinched Anna's cheek lightly.

"I don't know much," Anna said. "But I'll tell you, if you cross your heart not to tell."

"No, Anna. My word is better than that!" Kate held up her right hand. "I give you my word that I'll keep your secret."

"All right," Anna said in a half whisper. "When my mother first came here, she told me that she had left because she had a fight with Josh. He never hurt her, 'cept with words."

"Where is she, then?" Kate asked.

"She couldn't tell me. But she said I shouldn't worry, and soon she would make things right, so we could all be together."

"That's it?" Kate asked, somewhat disappointed. "That's all you know?"

"She asked about my bad dreams, and if I lost any more teeth . . . stuff like that."

"How does she get into the house?"

"Mama has a key."

"She just unlocks the front door?" Kate asked in astonishment.

"No, silly! She uses the back door."

"Why did she come up to my room today?"

"How do you know she did?" Anna asked.

"I smelled her lavender. Was she looking for something?"

Anna shrugged. "Maybe she wanted to meet you. She asks me about you."

"What does she ask?" Kate asked vehemently.

Anna became restless. "Oh, Kate! I can't remember all of it. Can I go to bed now? I'm so tired. Next time she comes, I'll tell her you'll help. You can meet her."

Kate helped Anna down from the bed. Ruffling the child's hair lightly, Kate laughed. "That's fine, now get off to bed!" As Anna sprinted down the hall, Kate whispered out to her, "Sleep well, Anna!"

That night Kate certainly slept soundly, relieved that Josh Redfield was definitely not a murderer. Joanna was alive! Now that her confidence in Josh was restored, Kate also noted that again Margo had been right.

She kept busy. Smoothly running a large house was no simple job, and teaching Lydia added to her burden. Nightly Kate thanked God for the patience He'd blessed her with, because somehow Lydia had a knack for knowing how to totally botch up any task. Kate learned early that she had to supervise her whenever she performed any task for the first time. Sometimes her student became frustrated and cried, making Kate feel like a jail warden, rather than a teacher.

Kate persisted. She had made up her mind to help Lydia, and she would stick to that. Geoffrey visited often now, but Kate stayed as far from him as she could. She didn't want him comparing her and his betrothed.

After a lengthy visit from Geoffrey one evening, Lydia bounded up to Kate's room with excitement.

"Guess what?" she asked, sinking into one of the chairs.

"I can't imagine," Kate answered without looking up from *Pride and Prejudice*.

"You aren't paying attention." Lydia stamped her foot, pouting. "Don't you want to hear a compliment?"

Kate sighed and lowered the book. "I'll give you five minutes."

"Geoffrey loves my new hairdo. He didn't care for the other styles as much as this one. Can you show me how to do it myself? Do I really look better this way?"

Because Lydia's face was so round, Kate had pulled her hair away from her face, tied it up high at the back of the head, and let the lifeless locks cascade down her back. Loose tendrils of hair hung beside her ears, softening her features.

"Of course, that's the easiest of them all to do. I'll show you how tomorrow. Anything else?"

"He's invited me to Thanksgiving dinner in Victoria. Do you think I might go for the day?"

"As long as you're back by bedtime, I see no problem with it," Kate replied with a yawn.

"What will *you* do for Thanksgiving? Won't you need my help?" Lydia asked with concern.

"We'll manage. Josh and I have agreed that celebrating the holiday season, with Joanna missing and all, would not be in good taste. We planned a simple Thanksgiving and Christmas. The only reason Josh wants to celebrate at all is for Anna."

"I'm glad my spending the day at Victoria won't inconvenience you. I'll say good night, and you can finish your book. By the way, thank you for everything. I owe you quite a bit, my friend."

Kate smiled. "What are friends for? Good night, Lydia."

When the sound of Lydia's footsteps had faded, Kate brought the book back up to her face.

Not two minutes later a feeble knock on the door made Kate sigh. *Now what? Was that Lydia again? Or did Anna forgot to tell me something?* "Come in," she sighed, laying the book down on her lap.

Kate jumped, when, instead of a familiar person, a strange figure clad in a black-hooded cape flowed into the room. Throwing the hood back, the form revealed long, straight, and glossy hair. The blond-haired, blue-eyed Dresden doll smiled. "I'm Joanna Redfield. You must be Kate!"

15

Kate tried to stand, but her knees trembled so, she plopped back into the rocker. "Yes, I'm Kate," she replied breathlessly. Lavender scent invaded the room.

Why did this women frighten her? Kate tried to calm herself and took deep, silent breaths, all the while studying Joanna Redfield.

Considering the tall, slim figure with willowy arms and legs, Kate decided she had never seen a more beautiful woman. Large, sparkling blue eyes blinked at her from a perfectly shaped porcelain face. Her rosy cheeks dimpled with a smile. Joanna looked like an adult Anna.

"I hope I haven't frightened you," she said.

Kate's head spun with confusion. Why did she resent Joanna? *Could I feel disappointed because she isn't dead?* Kate scolded herself. "Won't you have a seat?" She pointed to the other chair.

As she watched Joanna gracefully take a seat, an inkling

of the truth came to Kate. *I enjoy being with Josh, and I don't want anything to take that away.* She and Josh had shared no fancy balls, fine dining, or romantic moments, but Kate had come to enjoy the daily life at Hannah House: Bible readings in the study, chores accomplished side by side, and discussions they'd had about Anna's needs. Now that his wife had returned, that must end.

Why I even forgot he had *a wife—once I learned not to worry that he'd killed her.* Confused, Kate frowned at her own emotions. *Surely I'm not in love with the man!* She shed the thought. No, it was simply the fact that his wife was alive that made her feel guilty. Again Kate scolded herself, and she pledged to try and patch things up with Joanna and Joshua, just as she had taught Lydia to be a better wife to Geoffrey.

God, help me, she prayed silently. *Why, Lord, are You using me to help everyone else find happiness? What about me?* Realizing her error, she added, *I'm sorry for being so selfish. Please give me the guidance to do Your will, amen.*

Kate smiled at the mysterious woman. "What can I do to help you?"

"Anna said you could be trusted," Joanna said meekly. "Is that true?"

"Of course it is. I love Anna. I'll do anything I can to help." Kate responded with confidence.

Joanna let out a sigh. "I'm so glad. I don't know who to turn to, who to ask for help. Will *you* help me, Kate?"

Kate studied the beautiful woman and, without planning to do so, envisioned Joshua folding his strong arms around this fragile girl and kissing her tenderly. Anger spurted up in Kate, and in those few seconds she gained more self-knowledge than ever before. And what she found didn't please her.

Kate had never loved Geoffrey Grandville. She'd only imagined a perfect relationship with him because he seemed to fill all the qualifications of a storybook hero. Josh Redfield had none of the worldly things she'd thought so important. Yet in her heart she knew she'd do *anything* to help him and Anna, because she loved them unconditionally.

Once Kate's mind was set, there was no changing it. With chin high she said, "Joanna, what can I do to help?"

"Talk to Arthur on my behalf," she asked anxiously.

"*Arthur*? Don't you mean *Josh*?"

"No, Arthur's the one who needs to forgive. Josh forgave me a long time ago and has spent the last seven years of his life helping me. I've been so selfish. Poor Josh!" She began sobbing into a handkerchief.

Kate broke in, "I'm confused. Can you tell me what this is all about?"

Joanna sniffled, blew her nose, and smiled feebly. "Arthur Redfield is my father."

Kate let this information digest before asking with bated breath, "You mean *father-in-law*?"

"No. Arthur is my father. Josh is my brother."

Kate fell back into her chair and almost laughed in relief. "Are you serious? You aren't Josh's wife?"

Joanna shook her head.

"What about Anna? Whom does Anna belong to?"

Joanna smiled. "Sit back and make yourself comfortable. I'll tell you the whole story. I need a friend to confide in. Can I call you a friend?"

Kate did laugh at that. "If you are truly Josh's sister and Arthur's daughter, you can call me anything you want!" Kate reached out and hugged the woman. "I'm so happy you aren't Josh's wife!"

Joanna winked knowingly. "I'd hoped that was the reason you felt that way. It will make my story easier to tell." Joanna sat back in her chair and idly played with her fingers. "Some of the things I tell you may shock you. Please bear with me until I'm finished, all right?"

Kate nodded.

"Many years ago my mother was involved in a carriage accident that left her partially crippled. The man who caused the accident was returning from a wild, all-night party. Mother had been taking me to London for a new dress that sunny morning. I don't recall much, except a jumble of screaming, the cries of the horse, wood splintering, and my mother frantically calling my name.

"The details of the carriage accident aren't important. But the drunken driver was the notorious Charles Barringer, who was known for his partying and knew how to make any get-together lively. His wife, Sara, stayed home and took care of their son, Phillip."

"*Phillip Barringer?*" murmured Kate. "Phillip Barringer is the man folks say you ran off with!"

Joanna nodded. "He's Anna's *real* father."

Kate gasped. "Honest?"

"Let me explain. Phillip and I met and fell in love. Though my father forbade me to see him, I could no more stay away from Phillip than I can Anna! I loved him.

"So I went to Josh for help. He always took care of his baby sister. This time I asked for too much, I'm afraid," she spoke mournfully.

"Josh had connections with a local church—he has always been spiritual—and arranged for Phillip and me to be married. We were both of age, so nothing could stop us. I was Phillip's wife for all of three days! Or should I say, until my father found out. He had a temper tantrum like never before. According to Josh, he threw furniture and broke dishes! Then he contacted a friend, a judge, I believe, and he drew up papers of annulment.

"It wasn't really legal, since neither of us was a minor, but my father did it anyway." Joanna's voice remained surprisingly mild. "To make certain, my father found and separated us and gave my husband a letter saying I wanted the annulment. Even when he saw the papers, Phillip didn't believe him. So my father had him beaten and drugged. The next thing I knew, I was husbandless and pregnant.

"Not only did Josh take the blame for the whole escapade, when I told him about the baby, he was burdened with guilt. Because he'd arranged the marriage, he felt that my condition was indeed his fault.

"You must understand, Kate, Josh and I had always been close. He was five years older and had always taken full responsibility for me." She sniffed into her handkerchief. "I love Josh!"

Joanna calmed herself and continued, "Josh discovered the truth, and we ran away to America to find Phillip. I gave birth to Anna in Philadelphia, before we even found Phillip's trail. It took us several years to finally locate him.

"Due to my condition and situation, Josh protected me by pretending to be my husband. We seldom ever had to actually lie; everyone just assumed our relationship, as they assumed Anna was his daughter. Even Anna thinks Josh is her father." For several moments Joanna wept into her handkerchief. "We were wrong, and our deception is not going unpunished.

"Finally Josh made contact with people from Victoria,

and we found Phillip. My brother and I settled here, and he started a lumber business, which has been extremely successful.

"After we made inquiries about Phillip, we stayed at a distance for some time, to be sure it was the Phillip Barringer we sought and that he had not married. I have to admit, too, that I felt hurt. Too many questions had bothered me for so long. Why had Phillip left me and never come back? Had he planned to live here without another thought for me? I had to be certain of his love.

"Once Phillip explained everything, I began to understand. I still had a lot to forgive him for—and he had to forgive *me* for all my doubts. It took a few months for our relationship to blossom here as it had in London. When we decided to remarry, we thought nothing stood in our way. We hadn't counted on Josh ever being a problem. Our remarriage didn't bother him, but my brother now loved Anna as a daughter. When I told him Phillip, Anna, and I were going to live on a ranch Phillip had purchased in Texas, Josh threw a tantrum. He became almost as irrational as Father. Phillip had to leave right away, or his deal on the ranch would fall through. He gave me an ultimatum: Go with him—with or without Anna—or lose him forever.

"Kate, I didn't know what to do! I loved them both! Then I watched Josh with Anna one morning, out by the garden, and I had my answer. I couldn't destroy the loving brother who'd given up seven years of his life for me. So I left with Phillip."

Kate sat spellbound by the intriguing story.

"When I say Josh sacrificed seven years for me, I mean just that. Often in our travels we met very attractive young ladies, and Josh couldn't even approach them for friendship. One young lady in New Orleans almost stole him away from me. Though he seemed amused by it, I know Josh would have loved to have made a life for himself, instead of living a bogus life with his own sister and niece.

"Josh truly loves Anna. But so do I! When we settled the paperwork and moved into our ranch in Texas, I couldn't be happy without her. I explained to Phillip how I felt, and he, too, wanted his daughter with us. Finally Phillip did what only the man I love would do: He sold the ranch to come back for Anna.

"We set up an appointment to talk it over with my father and Josh, but at the last moment, I lost nerve. I just cannot face my own father. So I came to Hannah House instead, knowing he'd be somewhere else, awaiting me.

"Phillip and I are prepared to begin our lives with Anna and Josh so that no one will be hurt. We will either build here near Josh or fulfill Josh's other dream and continue on to California.

"There is absolutely no reason Josh and Anna should not be together always." Joanna smiled. "Someday Josh'll marry and have children of his own. Then I'm sure they will take a larger part of his heart. Yet I can understand how he feels now."

Silence filled the room. Finally Kate spoke, "I agree with your decision. It seems fair, and I commend Phillip for giving up his ranch for Anna."

"That's why I love him. He is a good man." Joanna patted Kate's hand. "Can I give you advice? Forget how handsome or wealthy a man is. Look for a treasure in him that money can't buy and handsomeness can't replace—caring. Phillip cares, and because he does, I can always trust him to do whatever is right."

Kate smiled knowingly. "I believe I know exactly what you mean."

Joanna stood and flipped up her hood. "Will you help me?"

"Certainly," said Kate. "But just what do you want me to do?"

"Talk to my father—he's being so unfair, blaming Phillip for something he didn't do. If my father can't forgive my husband's family for what happened to Mother, he'll never allow us to be happy.

"It's not just Phillip and I," she added hesitantly. "My father also thinks Anna belongs to Josh, from a wife who died in childbirth." Joanna explained quickly, "We had to give him some answers, because he wanted to know why I stayed in America and who Anna was."

Joanna sighed. "We lied and deceived our father, but only complicated our lives. Once you begin telling lies. . . , there's no end. We dug our own graves, so to speak."

"What do you want me to tell Arthur?"

"Tell him the whole story, as I've told you. See if you can convince him to forgive and forget, so that each of us can live our own lives."

"I'll do that." Kate blurted, "But why don't you tell him yourself?"

"Because I'm afraid of him."

"Why doesn't Josh tell him?" Kate suggested. "Surely your father would feel more comfortable with a family member mentioning it than having a stranger like me talk to him about personal affairs."

"Because," explained Joanna, "Josh refuses to tell him. He says it's *my* secret, and he'll live with it and cover for me forever, if necessary. He claims that it's my secret to tell, not his."

"Exactly what are you afraid of?" Kate asked.

"My father has a violent temper, for one. I also fear what he could do. What if he sends Phillip away again or something? He has powerful friends, and there is no limit to his hatred for the Barringers."

"I found your locket," Kate said. "Why did it look as though someone had torn it off?"

"Because it was ripped off in anger—by me! When Josh refused to let me take Anna, I threw a fit, grabbed my locket, and threw it across the room. Later, on my way out, Joshua and I had words again, and I pressed my mother's ring into his palm. He'd given it to me as part of our ruse as a married couple."

Shaking her head in disbelief at how twisted minds had invented dramatic stories to fit the ring and how her own imagination had seen the locket ripped off Joanna's limp body, Kate felt ashamed. "I suppose," Kate questioned meekly, "that the argument people heard between Josh and Phillip was about Anna, not you?" At her puzzled look, Kate explained, "Josh was heard shouting at Phillip that he'd take her away over his dead body. Folks thought he meant *you!*"

Joanna smiled slightly. "And you thought that Josh had harmed. . . ?" She laughed. "He would never! Josh? You've got to be kidding!"

"Guilty as charged, Joanna," Kate said, blushing at her own ignorance.

Joanna sobered. "I suppose I'd think the same, in your place. After all, you do not know Joshua as I do." She twisted her hands nervously. "You'll still talk to my father for me?"

Kate walked Joanna to the door. "I'm not sure how, but I'll do something. I love Anna, too."

Joanna smiled. "I know you do. It shows. That's why I trust you." She kissed Kate on the cheek, opened the door, and drifted out into the darkness.

Sitting in the dark, illumined only by a faint glow from the fireplace, Kate contemplated the conversation with Joanna and planned her speech to Arthur Redfield. How could she present the facts to Joanna's father so that he would become sympathetic instead of hateful? One by one, Kate rejected impossible ideas, replacing them with no practical ones. *Even if I accomplished my goal, I have no way to let Joanna know.* The intense thought startled Kate. Where were Joanna and Phillip, and how could she contact them?

Unfinished thoughts swirled in Kate's head, causing her to toss and turn in her bed that night. Eventually sleep must have overtaken her, for a nightmare woke her with a jerk.

After recovering from the fright, Kate's relieved mind replayed the dream. Geoffrey Grandville had been running from the Redfield chicken hut, with a big, white chicken clenched between his unusually large teeth. Josh had surprised him from behind the house and held a shotgun pointed at him. Dropping the chicken, Geoffrey fell to his knees, begging for forgiveness.

She would never forget the look of agony on Geoffrey's face. Lydia had run out then, stood directly in front of Geoffrey, and cried bravely to Josh, "You'll have to kill me first."

"If I have to, I will," Josh answered.

Kate recalled her own voice, shouting, "No, you can't shoot someone for merely stealing a few birds. Perhaps Geoffrey was hungry. Don't shoot!"

Josh's finger had tightened on the trigger. "Someone has to pay for this with his own life! Which of you will it be?"

He aimed carefully at Geoffrey's heart, only inches from Lydia's temple.

Kate's voice echoed words she had so clearly spoken in the dream. Now she could practically see them written on the bare bedroom wall: "Someone has *already* died for every sin!"

16

When Kate awoke the next morning, she knew what had to be done. The dream had been silly, as most of hers were, yet it had given her an idea as to how she could reach Arthur. While she dressed and prepared for the day, she prayed for guidance.

Kate started the fire, and while the oven warmed, she made blueberry muffins and coffee. The smells seemed to draw a crowd, for in minutes the dining room was full of everyone except Arthur.

Josh had mumbled a tired "good morning," taken a sip of the coffee she had poured and set before him, and smiled. "That's great coffee, Katherine!"

Kate beamed at him as she scooped oatmeal from the saucepan to his bowl. She moved on to Anna's dish. "Anna," she scolded lightly, "why are you covering your bowl with your hands?"

"Don't want no oatmeal!" She pouted.

Josh gave her a stern look.

"I don't want *any* oatmeal," Kate corrected.

"Me either!" she cried with her bottom lip trembling.

"Anna?" Josh pronounced her name dangerously.

"You don't have to eat any," Kate replied sweetly.

Anna smiled and gave Josh a victorious look. "I don't?"

"Most certainly not. I'd never force anyone to eat. She might get sick." Kate picked up Anna's bowl and moved on to Lydia.

Lydia winked at Kate. "I'll eat Anna's share. I'm hungry as a bear!"

Kate divided the rest into Lydia's bowl and her own. She took the empty pan into the kitchen and poured cool water in it. When she returned, she poured Anna a small glass of milk. "Enjoy, Anna."

The child remained silent but smiled victoriously as everyone ate oatmeal. When Lydia and Josh had finished, Kate took their bowls into the kitchen and returned with hot blueberry muffins. She gingerly tossed one onto each plate except Anna's.

"If they're as tasty as they smell, we're in for a treat!" exclaimed Josh.

"M-m-m, my favorite," purred Lydia.

"Anyone want butter?" Kate uncovered the dish.

All three reached for the butter at once and let it melt onto their hot muffins. After biting into them, each person murmured appreciation.

"Hey!" cried Anna. "I'll have one of those, too!"

"But Anna," Kate sounded reasonable, "this is dessert."

"So what?" Anna cocked her head in puzzlement.

"Silly!" exclaimed Kate. "No one can have dessert if she hasn't eaten the meal. Everyone knows that! The dessert is the reward for eating what's good for you."

Josh smiled and agreed. "Everyone knows that!"

Lydia nodded. "And this is the best reward I've ever had. Could I have another, Kate?"

"No." Kate said firmly. "You may not!"

"Why? Are they all gone?" Lydia asked sadly.

"No, I have plenty."

Even Josh looked at her in puzzlement.

"Why not?" Josh and Lydia chorused.

"Because," Kate said firmly, "you're my friend."

"What? I don't understand," Lydia objected.

"Lydia, you asked me to help you look good for Geoffrey. That's why I won't let you have another muffin. You must begin watching how much you eat!"

Lydia pouted silently, as if trying to decide if she should kiss Kate or knock her down and grab another muffin. Finally she looked up sheepishly. "You're right. I'll start making the beds instead. Thanks, Kate!" She blew her a kiss and dashed up the stairs.

Only a sulking Anna and an astonished Josh remained at the table with Kate. Josh gave Kate a look of wonder and started to say something, but Anna cut him off. "I'll have my oatmeal now," she said sweetly. "I wasn't very hungry before, but I think I am now."

"I did put some aside for your grandfather. I suppose I could let you have his—"

"Oh, please!" Anna cried. "And save me a muffin, too!"

Josh's eyes twinkled as he looked at Kate with true appreciation.

Kate brought Anna a bowl of steaming oatmeal and set it before her. The little girl gobbled it down.

"Kate," Josh said. "There's something I'd like to discuss with you. Can you come into the den for a moment?"

"Sure," she replied, gathering dishes and starting for the

kitchen with them, "as soon as I take Arthur his breakfast. Go on ahead; I'll meet you there."

Kate carefully balanced the breakfast tray on her shoulder and climbed the stairs to Arthur's room. She knocked lightly.

"What?" he growled.

"It's Kate. I have your breakfast. May I come in?"

"About time! I'm starving to death up here!" he yelled.

Kate opened the door, walked carefully to the bedside table, and lowered the tray. "Sorry, I had problems getting Anna to eat this morning—"

"No wonder! What's this? Gruel?"

"No, it's oatmeal," she replied sweetly.

"I don't want that stuff—" He reached for the muffin.

"Oh, no you don't," she cried. "No oatmeal, no muffin!"

He sighed with frustration. "You're just like Hannah! A blasted nursemaid bossing her charge!"

Kate removed the muffin from his tray and started for the door.

"Where do you think you're going with that?" he bellowed.

"I'm taking it back to the kitchen until you eat your oatmeal."

"Don't treat me like a child," he snapped. "Bring it back." In a low tone he added, "I'll eat the gruel."

She watched as he ate, wondering how to soften such a hard-boiled egg as Arthur Redfield.

"Arthur, do you remember the crucifixion story?"

"The what?"

"Crucifixion. You know, when they put Christ on the cross."

"Of course!"

"I've always liked the part where Jesus forgives the thief on the cross beside Him. Do you remember?"

"Ah-huh," he murmured as he ate his oatmeal.

"What a wonderful lesson for us all. Christ showed us how He'd like us to treat our fellowman. If Christ, in his perfect state, could forgive a worthless thief and promise him a place in heaven, then surely we can—"

"That won't work!" Arthur bellowed. "Hannah tried that on me years ago. Let me tell you something, miss; I watched the only woman I ever loved slowly melt away. There is no way I can ever forgive the Barringers—so don't even try to make me." He pointed to the door. "I'd like to eat in peace. I've a headache, remember?"

Kate shrugged and walked from the room, defeated. Going to her room, she plopped herself upon the bed. There had to be a way to reach Arthur Redfield! She'd just have to find it.

Lost in thought, Kate jumped when a knock fell on her door. "Yes?" she called.

The door opened and Anna barged in, waving a paper. "I want to show you what I made for my mother."

Kate smiled and reached for the paper. After studying it, she looked at Anna, puzzled. "Anna, what does this mean? An eye, a heart, and the letter U?"

"I love you!" exclaimed Anna proudly. "I thought of it myself."

"But why didn't you just write it? Now your mother will think me a poor teacher. She'll wonder why you cannot write those words."

"Mama knows I can. I've done it for her. I need to tell her I love her in a stronger way."

"Stronger way?" Kate asked.

"Grandfather told me that words don't mean beans if you

don't do something. I'll give her a big kiss; then give her this."

Kate smiled. "Did he say, 'Actions speak louder than words'?"

"Yes, that too!"

"Interesting." Ideas formed in Kate's mind. "So he said that, did he?"

"Josh is still waiting for you in the den. He said I should remind you, if I saw you—"

"Oh! I forgot!" Kate leapt from the bed and ran down the stairs. When she finally reached the den, it was empty.

"Drat!" she stamped her foot. *I wonder what Josh wanted?* A rustle at the door caused her to spin around. "Oh, Josh! I'm sorry . . . I was held up in Arthur's room—he was playing games with his breakfast, much like Anna."

"I just left to answer the door. It was Margo," he said, taking a seat beside the warm fireplace and motioning for her to sit across from him. "I told her I wanted a few words with you, so she's visiting Lydia first."

Kate took a seat opposite him and folded her hands in her lap expectantly.

Josh smiled. "Katherine, you amaze me! You run this household as well as Ayda and handle Anna better than Joanna!"

Kate noticed how his eyes sparkled when he was pleased.

He continued, "I don't know quite how to begin this conversation. But I'd like to apologize for my stupidity and inability to speak. I know what I want to say, but the words come hard. Since problems don't go away when I ignore them, I may as well face and deal with them.

"When you were invited to Hannah House, I knew you must have heard the gossip around town about me. The fact that you accepted my invitation proved to me that you paid it no heed—or perhaps you simply came despite the horror stories. It won you points with me, though. I thought you tough and adventurous.

"Your first day here I should have had this talk with you, but . . . I put it off." He squirmed a bit. "I'm not much of a conversationalist." His eyes seemed to plead for a response.

"You're doing fine," she smiled encouragingly.

"Anyway, I'll get to the point. I've invited you here under false pretenses, because I am not Anna's father, but her uncle." He looked at her expectantly. "Not surprised?" His eyes widened.

"Go on . . . ," she prompted.

He took a deep breath. "Anna is the product of my doing, but not directly. . . . I mean—that isn't what I meant to say. . . . What I mean is she—my sister, Joanna, rather . . . ," he faltered.

Kate came to the rescue. "Relax, Josh, I've already spoken with Joanna."

"You have?" He looked at her as if she'd given him a pleasant surprise. "And you let me muddle through this horrid, embarrassing story!"

Nodding, Kate said, "I enjoyed every minute of it. You deserved it, you know, for not having this conversation with me that first day."

"What spunk! That's another word to fit you, Katherine. You're tough and spunky." Josh sobered somewhat and added softly, "I like you. Like you a lot."

Kate looked down, blushing. As she peeked up at him again, her heart pounded loudly.

"I thought about everything at breakfast this morning and knew I'd been wrong." Josh looked deep in her eyes. "You've been wonderful, and I haven't been truthful. I'm glad you knew the story, so I didn't have to go into detail."

"Joanna has asked me to speak to Arthur on her behalf. I told her that I would, but I haven't made any headway. Your father is awfully stubborn."

"That's only one of his admirable qualities."

Kate told him about the approach she'd tried that morning.

Josh shook his head. "Words can't penetrate his thick skull."

Kate sighed. "Joanna and Phillip deserve a life with their daughter, and they are willing to compromise—Why do they need Arthur's consent? Since you don't object, why don't they just live as a family?" Kate asked.

"My father generally has a quick temper, but about this he acts almost insane. He's very protective of Joanna. Why, to get rid of this new son-in-law, he even hired men to club Phillip over the head, drug him, and put him aboard a ship. Phillip had money in his pocket and a letter from my father, threatening his life and Joanna's, if he returned."

"Are you sure Arthur would react violently, if he knew the whole truth?" she queried.

"He knows. I told him the first day you came. Remember our talk in the den all that evening? He hardly left his room the next day. He has already threatened all sorts of things." Josh stood up and began pacing nervously. "He did lie about one thing, though."

Kate looked up at him with one raised eyebrow.

"He said that night he'd have nothing more to do with Anna, because she was a Barringer. No matter how hard he tried, he couldn't hurt Anna. He loves the child dearly, whether or not he admits it. I'm sure he's mellowed somewhat with age, because years ago he would have completely ignored the girl."

Josh laughed. "That very next evening Anna crawled up on Arthur's lap and asked him to play checkers with her. He melted like butter on a desert cactus."

Kate held up her hand. "I had an idea this morning, but I need some help perfecting it. Are you interested?"

"Idea on what?"

"On how to reach Arthur and get him to forgive the Barringers."

"Yes, I'd love to hear it!"

"You promise not to laugh? It's pretty farfetched."

Josh held his hand up solemnly. "I promise."

17

*K*ate pointed to the chair across from her. "Please? Now, are you ready for my idea?"

Josh nodded. "Ready."

"I know you'll think I have an overactive imagination! Maybe it comes from all the reading I do—I always have my nose in a novel. Just tell me if you think this idea is too dramatic for the real world."

He winked. "I think I like your imagination and your quick wit. I promise to be fair."

"This morning Anna came into my room with a colorful picture of a huge eyeball, a heart, and the letter U," Kate began. "She claims that her grandfather told her words are meaningless without action—or actions speak louder than words. So she drew an action picture, of 'I love you' and explained that she planned to present the picture to her mother, with a kiss."

Josh nodded impatiently.

"We take Arthur's advice. Words, to him, are futile; we

need to show him. I thought of a way to prove how foolishly he's acting."

"Sounds logical so far. Go on," Josh prodded.

"We could try to arrange a way that Phillip could save your life or Joanna's—wouldn't that repay the debt to your father? Or perhaps we could have him save *Arthur's* life!" She folded her hands in her lap and looked at him expectantly. "What do you think?"

Josh sat silently and rubbed his temples for so long that Kate thought it took him minutes to answer her.

"Your idea has merit, Kate. Why doesn't my mind think of schemes like those? You could write a good book, with all that imagination!"

"I've thought about it. Perhaps someday." Kate played with the folds of her dress. "But are you willing to try it?"

He looked at her thoughtfully. "I like the idea, but am afraid my father would see right through a life-saving attempt. Don't you think so?"

She pondered it for several moments. "He is awfully sharp, isn't he? It would have to be very well done."

"And," added Josh, "he has a devious mind—not merely creative, like yours, but downright devious. He'd see through it like a sheet hanging on a clothesline at noon."

Kate laughed. "You lied."

"About what?"

"You said you had a hard time saying things. I like your way with words!"

He blushed. "Thank you."

"So I'll think of another plan then?" she asked in a voice tinged with disappointment.

"I didn't say we wouldn't try it, only that I felt my father was too smart to fall for any simple plan. It's certainly worth considering."

He rose. "Let's work out the details and meet here again tomorrow at this time, to compare notes. How does that sound?"

She smiled and held out her hand. "Partners?"

"Partners." He shook her hand firmly.

The sound of laughter coming from Lydia's room reminded Kate of Margo's presence in the house. She tapped lightly and opened the door. "What's all this?" she exclaimed at the packages strewn about the room.

"Lydia's wedding dress!" Margo danced about, holding it up to herself. "Isn't it the final word?"

Kate reached out and touched the delicate lace. "It's the loveliest material I've ever seen. Wherever did you get such a fine dress, Lydia?"

"I had it made in New York. My father sent it by stage."

Kate's eyes filled. "You'll make a beautiful bride. I'm so happy for you—" She broke away and fled to her room. Throwing herself on her bed, she berated herself, *Why couldn't you control yourself? Now what will you tell them? Margo and Lydia will think you're jealous. Are you?* She wept silently and didn't even know why.

Within minutes Margo knocked at her door and called her name. Kate wiped her eyes and blew her nose.

"Open the door, Kate, it's Margo."

Kate swept a book out from under the bed and curled up with it. "Come in, door's open."

Margo and Lydia pushed their heads through the door cautiously and peered around before entering. "What are you doing?" asked Margo.

"Reading."

"Why did you run from us in tears?" Lydia asked.

"You know how romantic I am? Those type of things choke me up, that's all."

"Well, you certainly gave us a scare!" scolded Margo. "We thought for sure something was horribly wrong."

"Things have never been better. How are the twins?"

"Fine. They didn't get measles, but they're getting on my nerves. I can't wait for school to open again. It keeps them occupied."

"Have you heard anything from Mr. O'Brien?"

"No. He said he'd let me know, so I suppose he doesn't think school should resume yet."

"Have any more children come down with measles?"

"Just one that I know of—Effie Groom."

"I almost *went* there!" Kate cried.

"I'm terribly concerned for poor Olive," said Margo.

"Why? Is she ill, too?" pressed Kate.

"In a way, yes."

"What's wrong?" Lydia asked with concern.

"I can't say, except she isn't as healthy as she looks, and she does her housekeeping poorly because she's ailing most of the time."

"A secret disease, is it?" Kate mocked.

"In a way it is!" Margo defended Olive. "She suffers from continual low spirits.

"That's as much as I can tell you." Anger sparked in her voice. "Just remember her in your prayers. Don't let what others tell you about Olive Groom shade your opinion of her. I knew her when she first married, and her house was one of the cleanest in all of Hays!"

"I'm sorry, Margo. I didn't mean to sound uncaring." Kate put her arms around the other woman. "I'll pray for Olive. I'm so proud that you're my friend, and I'm going to try to be more like you."

"Me, too!" Lydia cried, rushing in to embrace them both. "You both are inspirations to me."

Kate broke the embrace and spoke firmly to Lydia. "It's time to start lunch. You go on ahead, and I'll join you. I haven't had a chance to visit with Margo alone yet."

"But what should I do?" asked Lydia.

"Start boiling some water, and preheat the oven. Make coffee, the way I showed you, and take out the butter. By the time you do all that I'll be there with you."

When Lydia had gone, Kate sighed. "Well, Margo. She's coming along just fine."

"Really?" Margo looked surprised. "Is she really doing well?"

"At first I nearly pulled my hair out. If there was a way to botch the job I gave her, she found it! Thank the Lord for His gift of patience, because that's all it took. Lydia is not stupid, just a slow learner. Once she catches on, she doesn't forget and follows orders to a tee! Don't worry, she'll be the perfect Mrs. Geoffrey Grandville."

"Thank you, Kate. I really didn't think you'd give it your best. I mean, you seemed so reluctant to even try teaching Lydia. I thought you disliked her for some reason. This news is really wonderful!" She kissed Kate's cheek. "You know, you're a good friend to have, too!"

Kate laughed. "How do you like Lydia's new hairdo?"

"It's perfect! Geoffrey told me about it! He's noticed many changes in Lydia. Things he'd secretly worried about. You've helped them become perfect for each other. God will certainly bless you, too, Kate. Wait and see!" Margo said, pointing her finger at Kate. "You wait and see what wonderful thing He'll do for you!"

"I feel good about myself, Margo, that's all the reward I need. I've learned so much since I came out here." Kate chuckled. "And I thought I was coming here to *teach* rather than *learn!*"

Margo gave her a knowing look. "We never stop learning, my dear, never."

The next morning, after breakfast, Kate met Josh in the den.

"Well." She laughed. "Have you smoothed out the ripples in our crooked scheme?"

"Of course. I've even talked to Joanna and Phillip. Joanna was elated and claims she knew she could trust you to solve the problem. She thinks you have some secret quality—of course, who am I to argue with her, right?"

"Exactly." Kate's eyes sparkled gleefully.

Josh looked at her intently, his brown eyes twinkling. "You *do* have an unusual quality. Something magnetic." She had to strain to hear his next words, for he turned away and spoke under his breath. "And I'm a helpless piece of metal."

Kate blushed, and her insides lurched as they never had before. It seemed as if senses she'd never felt before suddenly came alive. She blinked. "Seriously?"

He nodded. "I may just inspire you enough to write a story of your own."

"I think you could" was all she said, shaking off the mood. "What ideas have you come up with? Where do we begin and when?"

"You're the creative one, what have you come up with?"

"Do you suppose we could get Arthur to ride Loco? When he starts spinning, we could arrange to have Phillip there just in time." Kate gave Josh a doubtful look. "I know it's not great, but it's all I could come up with."

Josh considered for several seconds. "It might work, if we

knew where and when Loco would spin. But getting him to ride that horse after what happened to you would be almost impossible."

"Again you're right." Kate sighed mournfully. "Why do we have such a hard time helping Arthur think well of a good man? After all, Phillip's hardly the image of his father. He must have so many fine qualities. We just have to show them to *your* father."

"Making my father see good in a Barringer is almost impossible!" A grim look appeared on Josh's face.

"Too bad you don't have a few wild Indians here. Why, if Anna disappeared with them, Phillip could come to the rescue." Kate sighed. "But what are we to do, when you don't have any convenient savages?"

At her teasing look, Josh simply looked pensive.

"I suppose we have completely ruled out Phillip's saving you or Joanna?" Kate asked.

"My father would see right through that. Phillip thought so, too. We'd have a better chance at convincing him if we made it personal."

"What ideas have you come up with?" she asked.

"Only one, and it isn't as clever as yours." Josh winked. "And more dangerous and expensive, too."

"I can tell already it's more elaborate and better than my idea. What is it?" she asked.

"Remember that building behind the lumberyard?"

Kate nodded and recalled the first school site Margo had shown her.

"I could ask him to assist me in doing some work in it." Josh chuckled. "I hadn't thought yet what I'd have him do, but something that would leave him alone in it long enough for it to catch fire."

"Fire!" exclaimed Kate. "That *is* dangerous! What if someone should get hurt?"

Josh nodded. "See what kind of ideas an uncreative man gets?"

"Is that your only idea?" she asked.

"I'm afraid so. I'll talk to Phillip later today or tomorrow and see if he has any ideas. Then we'll give Joanna a vote. How's that sound?"

"Perfect! I can't wait to begin." A mischievous glint lit her eye.

"You are enjoying this, aren't you, Katherine?"

"Why do you call me that?"

"Katherine? It's your name, isn't it?"

"Yes, but no one calls me that unless I'm in trouble. Until now, that is!"

"And now?"

"It . . . it sounds more personal."

"That's because I'm the only one who calls you that. Do you want me to stop?" he asked, reaching for her hand and moving near.

Kate's head spun. Could Josh be interested in her? All the time she'd suspected him of evil, had he cared for her? She'd never have suspected this emotion lay behind his facade.

Is this my Romeo? she wondered as his face hovered over hers. *A man who owns a lumberyard and can't even tell me how he feels?*

His lips met hers, and instinctively Kate took a step backward. "Why did you do that?" she asked, once he'd drawn away.

"To show my appreciation for all you've done and—"

"A 'thank you' would have been adequate!" she snapped, turned on her heel and fled the room. As she ran up the stairs she scolded herself, *It's you, not him, that backed away. Why did you jump at the chance to alienate him? You know he had more to say, yet you cut him short and left him feeling like a dolt! Katherine Marie Hunter! Do you know yet what you want?*

Once into her room she locked the door and peered at herself in the mirror. *Just what do you want, Kate? To forever read of love for others? Why, after all these years of reading about romance, do you shy away when it comes into your own life? What are you afraid of?*

18

*I*t was a beautiful, crisp, late-fall day, and the schoolhouse was full for Sunday services, despite the measles. Kate noted that a few of her pupils who'd first contracted the disease were in church and healthy.

Once Kate had apologized to Josh for her behavior the night before, the only problem they had was getting Arthur to accompany them to church. Josh finally asked Anna to plead with her grandfather, and Arthur reluctantly agreed to come. He covered what he thought would look like weakness by saying, "You can make me go with you, but you can't make me stay awake!"

Kate wore a crisp, dove-gray dress with matching gloves and hat, while Lydia came down wearing a blue-and-white outfit with a violet hat. After a reminder from Kate, she changed to a violet dress, to better match the bonnet, because she couldn't find a blue or white hat.

As was usual in fair weather, when the services were over, the people gathered in groups outside the schoolhouse. Children ran in and out, between the adults, playing as much as possible in their short time together. Kate carried on a conversation with Lydia, Geoffrey, Archie Kessler, and Clara Haun, while Joshua talked animatedly with Buzz and Nancy Balcomb. Hester O'Neill had Arthur sequestered in a corner and seemed to be filling his ears with the latest gossip. Ayda Simcox, Margo, and Elmer laughed heartily over something Luther Aldrich had said. As Kate listened to Geoffrey tell a hunting story, she found her eyes searching out Joshua Redfield. Their eyes met, and he smiled and signaled her by looking at his watch and raising his eyebrows, as if to say, "Shall we go home and eat dinner?"

Kate nodded, and he exaggerated a lip pantomine that told her to find Anna.

Excusing herself from her group, Kate went in search of the child, whom she'd seen not five minutes ago, playing with the Dutton twins. As she scanned the area for Anna's red and green dress, she located every other child but Anna.

She walked up to Arthur, who was still busy listening to Hester O'Neill. "Have you seen Anna?" Kate interrupted.

He held up his hand, signaling her to wait, as Hester was in the middle of a heated sentence, her hand covering her mouth discreetly.

So no one will know she's gossiping! Kate supposed.

Kate sighed. "Well, bring Anna to the carriage. Josh wants to leave."

Nodding his head, Arthur kept his ears with Hester, but his eyes scanned the area for his granddaughter.

Kate walked nonchalantly toward Josh and the carriage.

As he held the door open and assisted her inside, Josh whispered, "You don't look like a writer today."

"No?" she asked in surprise.

He shook his head with a positive look. "No, you look like an angel or a saint in that conservative but lovely dress."

She blushed. "If that's a compliment, I accept it. Thank you," she said, taking her seat within the carriage, used only on special occasions and Sundays.

Holding the door patiently, Josh sent impatient glares Arthur's way. Arthur looked confused. Between trying to listen to Hester, soothe his anxious son, and look for Anna, he had more than he could handle. Ayda spotted his dilemma and came to his rescue by diverting Hester O'Neill. Other carriages were pulling away, and everyone seemed to be waving and well-wishing others. Adults rounded up children, who still darted about.

At first confusion covered Arthur's search, but soon he began yelling, "Anna! You come here this instant! Anna!" When he got no response, he stamped his foot in anger. Approaching the carriage, he commanded, "Go find your niece, Joshua! I'm not having any luck."

A few people near Arthur Redfield had overheard his remark to Josh. Suddenly a Babel arose: "Niece! Did you hear that?" "Isn't she his daughter?" "Surely the old man must be mistaken." "But wouldn't he know about his own family?" Yet no one dared confront Arthur.

None of the Redfields had time to deal with that problem now.

"Seems to me," Kate offered, "that I saw her with the Dutton twins, not five minutes ago, by that tree."

Josh marched off in the direction of the twins. Then Arthur and Kate watched him talk to several others, who passed along the word. Before five minutes had passed, panic had broken out, and everyone had forgotten the latest gossip about Josh.

"Anna's missing!" Berta Aldrich cried. "Someone check the creek!" Several men raced in that direction. Nancy Balcomb offered to search the nearby stables, and Carlton Haun and Mary Jane ran to check the nearby fields. Everyone could be heard calling her.

Arthur seemed ready to panic. "I'll make that child sorry, when we find her. See if I play checkers with her today! She's getting just like her mother. Has a mind of her own; does as she pleases with no mind for the consequences." He rambled.

"Has she ever done this before?" Kate asked, wringing her handkerchief.

"No and she never will again, if I have anything to say about it!" he bellowed.

Finally, when no Anna turned up, Josh drove Kate and Arthur back to Hannah House. As they got out of the carriage, "My greatest fear has materialized," Josh said sadly. "One of the Dutton twins saw Anna talking to a couple driving a buckboard, and when he looked again, Anna and the wagon had disappeared. I know it was Joanna and Phillip." Convincingly, Josh turned his back and rubbed his face. Then, he turned around and asked helplessly, "What do I do now? Where do I look?"

"You have to do something!" shouted Arthur.

"The men in town are searching, but I know they won't find her. Phillip and Joanna are probably miles away already." Josh pounded his fist on the carriage roof. "What will I do without Anna?" Josh's face looked as red and angry as his father's.

"Let's go inside!" Arthur ordered. "Going to pieces won't help. We have to think!"

Josh and Arthur paced the floor in the den while Kate served tea. She took a seat in a far corner and watched and listened tensely.

"It's your fault, Father." Josh pointed his finger at the old man. "Don't deny it. You forced Joanna and Phillip to stoop so low as to kidnap their own daughter."

"You don't know that for certain," he growled. "You're taking the word of an imaginative child. Perhaps she's just wandered off into the woods. Besides, how could those two come that close to the schoolhouse without anyone else seeing them and recognizing Joanna?"

"Easy!" shouted Josh. "Everyone knows how confusing it is when church lets out! And Carl Dutton said they used the road in back of the church. The one we use, which runs just from our Hannah House to the school. Only a few playing children were behind the building. Carl claimed they pulled off close to the woods, and Anna ran out to meet them."

"How do you know it wasn't some other kidnapper? What makes you so sure it's your sister and that— that—"

"Come on, Father. Wake up! You know they had no other alternative. Because of *your* stubbornness, they had to steal their own daughter. Do you know how many nights I lost sleep, fearing this?"

Arthur Redfield stamped his foot. "Confound it! Do you think you're the only one that's heartbroken? What about me? I loved the little. . . ." His voice broke, and he quickly turned his back.

Josh remained silent.

Arthur blew his nose before turning to face his son. He

shrugged. "It's done. How can we change things? I'll do whatever you say."

"Honestly? Do I have your word?"

"Of course! Do you think I wouldn't help recover my own granddaughter?"

"We can't simply steal her back, you know. We have to negotiate with Phillip and Joanna—if we can find them, that is. Will you forgive Phillip, so he and Joanna can settle nearby with Anna and let us share her life?"

Arthur hesitated. "I have to do *what*?"

"Forgive Phillip and his family. Formally. For once and for all time."

Arthur paced.

"Well?" Josh insisted.

"You're sure they are the ones who took her?" he asked.

"Yes, I'm sure. Why else couldn't we find her?"

Arthur continued to pace nervously.

"Yes or no?" prodded Josh.

"After all," Arthur reasoned, "it isn't as if it were Phillip who drunkenly hit Hannah. It's the same as if *I* were to be held responsible for something *you* did. I suppose I could forgive Phillip. . . ." He faltered, looking at his son sheepishly.

"Sign here." Josh whisked out a legal-looking document.

"W-what?" Arthur was taken aback. "What is that?" he asked suspiciously. "Why did you have it all ready for me to sign?"

"I drew up this agreement when I first learned you were coming here to visit. Joanna helped me write it. I carried it to church, because I hoped today's sermon about forgiveness might touch your heart. I have carried it daily, in hope that you'd reconsider," Josh explained.

"Why do I have to sign? Isn't my word good enough?"

"Not when you've carried a grudge this many years."

"How do I know we'll get Anna back, if I sign this?"

"You don't. But if we *don't* find her, we don't get to use this agreement anyway, so no harm done."

Arthur reached for the pen Josh held. He grabbed it and scribbled his signature on the line Josh had indicated. "Now, how do we find Anna?"

"Some of the men from town have ridden out and are searching all trails leading south to Texas. We merely wait." Josh folded the agreement, winked at Kate, and took a seat beside her. "Would you like some dinner, Father?"

"No. This tea is enough." He began pacing again. "I'll never forgive myself if Anna isn't found," he said in a shaky voice. "I admit it. *I was wrong.*" He spun around quickly for a man of his age. "Did you both hear me? *I was wrong,*" he repeated. "What else can I do?" he asked frantically.

Kate took pity on the old man. "Pray," she whispered to him. "That's all we can do now."

"And be thankful," Josh remarked curtly.

"Thankful?" Both Arthur and Kate asked at once.

"Yes. Be thankful that God is more forgiving than you are, Father."

"You're right again," the chastened old man bowed to Josh. "I'll be in my room, making my peace with God. If there's any word, please call me at once."

Josh nodded curtly to the vanishing figure. Then he shook his head sadly. "Forgive me, Lord," he whispered. "And thank You."

Kate watched him. "What's that about? Why do you need forgiveness?"

"Because I haven't been totally honest. Yet I feel God

understands that I only meant good. Perhaps that's why He let this mismanaged plot work." Josh's eyes glittered with joy.

"I don't understand," she said with a puzzled look. "How can you be happy, when Anna is still missing? A few moments ago you were crushed. . . . Now just because your father agreed to forgive, you're elated. But if Anna's not found . . . , what have you accomplished?"

Josh laughed. "But I know exactly where Anna is!"

"You do?"

"Of course! Do you think I'd be standing here chatting, if I didn't know where she was? Do you think I'd trust those other men who are searching?" He laughed again. "I'd be riding like the wind toward Texas!"

"You *know*?" she gasped. Then with a suspicious look she added, "You planned this!"

He nodded.

"Without me? I thought we were partners?" she asked, hurt that she hadn't been included in the plot.

"But you're the one who gave me the idea. I couldn't have done it without you!"

"Me?" Kate asked.

"Certainly. Remember 'Actions speak louder than words'? That got me thinking. While I thought about plots to save Arthur's life, I got the idea. But if it hadn't been for your comment about needing Indians, I wouldn't have even thought of anything dramatic at all. It was all your doing!"

"Did you think I wouldn't feel upset over losing Anna?" She stamped her foot. "You could have clued me in. We were partners!" She walked toward the door, angrily. "I hope your plan works. Did you ever stop to think that maybe Phillip and Joanna will just forget about coming back to see if the scheme worked? Maybe they'll figure as long as they have Anna, why risk returning? Are you certain you know exactly where Anna is?" Kate asked, before closing the door on a perplexed Joshua Redfield.

19

*P*acing the floor of her room, Kate picked up a throw pillow from the rocker and tossed it against the wall. *How could Josh carry out a scheme without including me?*

How could I let myself fall for a deceiver like him? That man played up to me, gained my trust, and went off on his own. She grabbed the pillow again and smashed it against the wall.

Spinning around, Kate hugged the bedpost and gazed out the curved window. Leaves swirled in the wind. Soon snow would cover the ground. Would Thanksgiving bring knee-high snow, as it often had in Chicago?

A rapidly moving figure caught Kate's eye. The man on a cream-colored horse galloped toward the main road—Josh and Lumberjack? He must be seeking Anna!

Speeding across the house, to Ayda's room, Kate watched until the man and his mount became a small speck.

How had Joanna and Phillip hidden themselves? In Kansas you could be seen for miles, yet they had managed to get from the schoolhouse to a road leading south, with no one seeing them. Had everyone at the church been blind?

Kate sighed. At least the Redfields could live happily ever after. But what of her own life? Where would she go?

Resentment at the way Josh had treated her rose again. She picked up the ill-used pillow, only to realize, *I'm angry with him because I feel left out, not because he was wrong!*

I couldn't bear to have him ignore me again. It hurts to know he doesn't care for me!

Deep within, Kate understood that caring was not what she wanted from Josh. Though she cherished the way he considered her needs, that alone could never fill the void in her life.

Slowly she'd come to delight in having him by her in the commonplace things of life. She thought back to the shared breakfasts, the chores completed together, and the times they'd talked.

When I leave Hannah House, I won't even have that, Kate realized, and the thought made her stomach feel hollow.

Had she felt this way about Geoffrey? No, long ago she'd accepted that only romantic idealism tied her to the handsome Englishman. As soon as she'd seen a few of his minor shortcomings, she'd lost interest in him entirely. Kate had known Josh's flaws from the first, yet his basic goodness had still sneaked out and grabbed her attention.

Could she move in with another family, knowing it would cost her daily contact with the man she loved?

Disturbed by her own thoughts, Kate tried to distract herself. Returning to her room, she picked up *Malaeska: The Indian Wife of the White Hunter*, by Mrs. Ann Sophia Stevens. The dime novel was so exciting; she couldn't wait to finish it.

Tapping the volume gently in her palm, Kate began to

wonder if she'd taken the adventure and romance of her books too seriously. Look at the way they'd encouraged her to believe she loved Geoffrey!

I don't live in a novel, she realized. *I don't even want to. All the romance and adventure would mean nothing without Josh.*

What if he doesn't feel the same about me? The chilling thought was like an ice block on her heart. Nothing could ever force Josh to return her emotions.

I need to face reality, Kate decided. *When I put down a book, I have to leave it behind. I can't let it color my life so.*

Perhaps she should give up her favorite pastime. No, books sparked her imagination. *But God, not books, should control my life. He could provide the "perfect" mate. If He wants me to share my life with Josh, God can work that out.*

What if He willed that she should give up this love? Kate knew she'd need supernatural power. She knelt by her bed, as she had since childhood whenever she faced troubles. Forehead resting upon the mattress, she lost herself in prayer.

When she opened her eyes, the darkness of the room surprised Kate. She lit her lamp, picked up her Bible, and began to page through it.

A noise startled Kate. The Bible fell from her lap as she sprang up and scanned the room quickly. She gazed at the clock on the dresser: 9:20! She must have fallen asleep! A light knock on her door sounded familiar. That was what had awakened her! She frowned. Anna? No, she was gone. Arthur? She walked to the door and whispered, "Who's there?"

The soft response was too low for her to hear. Recognizing a woman's voice, Kate opened the door slightly and looked out. "Jo—" she started to exclaim, but the blond-haired woman gently slapped her hand over Kate's mouth. "Sh-h! Can I come in?"

Kate, still gagged by Joanna's hand, nodded eagerly.

Once inside, Joanna took her hand from Kate's mouth and threw back her black hood. "Surprised?" she asked. Her eyes looked red, and Kate guessed she'd been weeping.

All Kate's questions surfaced at the same time; unable to select one to ask quickly, she stood speechless.

"Sit down and tell me where you've been!" she ordered finally.

Joanna obeyed.

"Where is Anna? Does Josh know you're here?"

Joanna's smile vanished. "No one knows I'm here. Things have not gone as planned, I fear." She looked at Kate hopefully. "I need your help again."

"Of course, I'm here!"

"Did Josh tell you about our plan?" she asked.

Kate nodded.

"It's become terribly botched." She drew a handkerchief from her cape pocket and dabbed at her eyes. "Everything went as planned. We picked up Anna and headed for our destination—at the old dugout. Josh and I had agreed that we could tell Anna who her real father was when we got her there. He'd meet us later. So we fixed refreshments, and I told Anna the whole story, with Phillip looking on anxiously, beside me.

"When I told Anna, she wouldn't believe me! She began screaming and crying as I've never seen before! When her tantrum turned into hysterics, I became frantic myself." Joanna dabbed at her tearing eyes again. "What have I done to my daughter, Kate? Why did I ever begin this charade? I should have stood up to Arthur years ago!"

"Where is Anna now? Is she all right?" Kate asked anxiously.

Joanna sighed and went on with her story. "All I can think of is that not only was the truth too much for her, but she seemed to think we were never bringing her back—that she'd never see Josh again. Before we knew it, she'd darted out into the darkness, and we—" She cried into her handkerchief so that Kate could barely hear her. "We haven't been able to find her!"

"But Joanna," Kate exclaimed. "Why have you come to me? Shouldn't you be telling Josh?"

"I can't find him! I searched the whole house, and his horse isn't in the stable. Where is he?" she cried harder than before.

Kate looked at the clock. "He left here about seven o'clock, headed for the main road, and then turned east. I'd thought he'd gone to pick up Anna. Arthur agreed to forgive Phillip; he even signed a paper. I assumed—"

Joanna brightened. "*East* you say?"

Kate nodded.

"Oh, Kate, maybe he did head for the dugout! I came through the woods on foot, because I wanted to look for Anna. I could have missed him! If he went to the dugout, Phillip would tell him, and he's probably hunting for her, too!"

"Is there anything I can do?"

"Yes," Joanna sniffled. "Will you pray with me?"

Kate put her arms around the other woman. "Of course. That's exactly what is needed. We'll go downstairs, make a pot of tea, and pray until Josh returns with Anna."

Giving a trembling smile, Joanna looked at the clock. "He *must* be looking for Anna. Why else would he be gone so long?"

"That's exactly it," Kate comforted. "Now let's go downstairs, before our voices alert Arthur." Kate grabbed Joanna's hand and led her down to the sitting room.

Between sipping tea and praying, Kate and Joanna waited and listened for hoofbeats.

Kate had time to replay her conversation with Josh in her mind. "Oh, no!" she cried, startling Joanna.

"What? What is it?" Joanna cried, running to the window.

"I'm sorry. Please sit down. I just thought of something dreadful I'd said to your brother today. How could I have spoken so, even in haste?" Kate described her last conversation with Josh. "I can't believe my hurt feelings caused me to lash out at him. I clearly recall saying: 'I hope your plan works. Did you ever stop to think that maybe Phillip and Joanna will just forget about coming back to see if the game worked? Maybe they'll figure as long as they have Anna, why risk returning? *Are you certain you know exactly where Anna is?'* "

"But you had no way of knowing . . . ," Joanna offered.

"When will I ever learn to think before I speak? Please don't find an excuse for me, Joanna. I was a dolt."

She gave Kate a sympathetic look. "Perhaps we should have included you in our plan. But Josh was adamantly against it. He thought that your reaction to the plot would be more convincing to Arthur if it were genuine. You have no idea how worried Josh was that Arthur would call our bluff."

"But I should have—" Kate stopped short. "I hear a horse! Do you?"

They ran to the window, but neither could see anything in the darkness.

"C'mon," urged Kate. "Upstairs to Ayda's room. We can

see better in an upper, darkened room." Joanna raced behind her.

Within moments they received small visual hints of approaching riders. A belt buckle's glint from the sliver of a moon, a flash of a horse's eye, and vague, dark, shadowy figures against the somewhat lighter sky.

"There are at least two riders," Joanna said, with her nose pressed against the glass.

"They've ridden around to the stable. That means it has to be Josh and someone else." Kate pulled Joanna back downstairs with her. They waited patiently beside the back door, a kerosene lamp held high.

It seemed forever before figures approached the house. Finally Kate and Joanna let out a sigh of relief when Josh burst into the kitchen, carrying a sleepy child.

"Anna!" Joanna rushed forward, arms extended.

Josh placed the child into her grasp. Joanna rocked the half-awake girl and kissed her tenderly on the cheek. Motioning for her to put Anna to bed, Josh whispered, "We'll talk afterwards."

A few minutes later, when Lydia returned from her visit with Geoffrey at Victoria, they all filled her in on what had happened since that morning at church.

Joanna poured coffee while Kate cut the apple pie she and Lydia had made yesterday.

"What happened?" Josh asked his sister tenderly, as if knowing what she'd been through.

Joanna dabbed her nose with her handkerchief. "I explained to Anna that Phillip was her real father, and she went into hysterics. I've never seen her like that."

"Where did you find her?" Kate asked Josh.

"Find *her*? She found *me*!" he exclaimed. "I was on my

way to the dugout, to tell them about Arthur's agreement. About a half mile away, I spotted a weaving little figure, running frantically. I could barely believe my eyes. So I scooped her up onto my horse and held her sobbing, tired, and shaking little body. Luckily it wasn't so dark yet. I could see that big white bow in her hair, or I might not have recognized her at all.

"Then I found Phillip . . . , and here we are." He shrugged sadly. "Poor Anna."

"What have we done to her?" sobbed Joanna.

"She'll get over it," Kate comforted. She sipped her coffee. "Especially when she learns that Josh can still be a part of her life."

"Thank God," breathed Joanna. "We'll make her see that uncles are extremely special."

"How would you two like to build about a quarter of a mile from here?" Josh asked. "The land is yours, and so is the lumber. That's a better deal than you'll get anywhere."

Joanna looked up expectantly at Phillip, excitement sparkling in her blue eyes.

Her husband smiled. "Thank you, Josh. We accept. But I would like to make one small request." When Josh nodded, he continued, "I'd like as much time as possible with my daughter. We have a lot to make up for. I don't mean that you shouldn't see her, but if you could just give me a chance with her. . . ."

Josh threw his arms around Phillip. "Brother, it's the least I can do. After all, if I'm lucky, I'll be busy starting my own family!" He threw Kate a meaningful look.

Despite the initial shock, Kate found herself smiling. His remark thrilled her too much for her to hide her emotions. Had God answered her prayer?

Or was Josh speaking of someone else?

"Is there something we missed here?" Joanna's confused gaze flew from her brother to Kate several times, as if she were watching a Victorian tennis match.

He shrugged and had the grace to look embarrassed. "No, *I* missed the most important part. I haven't proposed yet."

As he saw Kate's face flush, Josh added, "This is rather personal. Don't you people have something else you could be doing—like turning in?"

Lydia smiled smugly. "It really is late." As she passed Kate she kissed her and whispered, "I knew it!"

A joyful Joanna pulled Phillip toward the stairs. "Good night everyone," she called loudly. To Josh she added softly, "I hope she says yes!"

When they'd disappeared, confusion overtook Kate. None of her romantic tales had prepared her for this moment.

Josh emptied the contents of the coffeepot into their two cups. He didn't seem much more at ease than Kate. "I'll explain," he said quickly. "Then you can . . . ," he faltered, then pushed on. "I wish I could say I fell in love with you from the moment we met. Your romantic novels probably say that's the way it should happen.

"I've never fallen in love before, and I guess it happened more slowly than that." He frowned to himself. "But despite that, I do love you, Kate. It sort of sneaked up on me, is all.

"I think it began when I knew you'd chosen our old home for the schoolhouse. Though all the gossips passed on their stories, you chose the best thing for your students. Even though you barely paid attention to me, I admired you for that stand. It took courage to risk the anger of some of the townspeople.

"Then I saw you with the children—especially Anna—and I knew you were one in a million. How many teachers would have cared so for one lost, hurting, little girl? The way you touched her heart seemed like a miracle.

"Of course I knew you hadn't eyes for anyone but Geoffrey Grandville. When I compared you to Lydia, I thought the man slightly foolish. Couldn't he see what he'd be missing? At the same time, I was glad, for it meant I had a chance to win your love. That's why I told you to take a chance at winning. I figured you would have to know sooner or later—and I couldn't bear to see you hurt too badly."

"I never loved Geoffrey, Josh," Kate comforted him. "I saw that soon after you told me to try to win his love."

Josh's eyes brightened, and he ran one hand through his hair. "I'm not good with words; you know that. I'm sorry for deceiving you about Anna's disappearance. I never meant to hurt you so. But I didn't want anyone to blame you for anything that happened, and I needed to have someone there who'd be as shocked as father, to make him believe it.

"If you'll marry me, Kate, I'll never deceive you again. I don't think I could bear to, after all the troubles we've had today. Why, if we'd lost Anna, I'd never have forgiven myself."

Kate's heart had been thumping wildly. She slowly nodded, and Josh took her in his arms.

"We'll build a small set of living quarters by the schoolhouse. . . ."

Confused, Kate looked up at him, doubt in her eyes. He had only just proposed. Did he already want to get rid of her?

"I want you to share my life at Hannah House, but it wouldn't be proper, now that we're engaged. Besides, the teacher who takes your place could use them, once we're wed. Though I think we need time to know each other better, I'm not going to wait forever, you know."

Kate laid her head on his shoulder. Strange, she thought, how real love didn't necessarily mean goosebumps and bells ringing. Hers had developed out of liking, then deepened slowly. Yet today she could hardly doubt her emotions as a thrill coursed from her head to her toes.

This was exactly what she'd been waiting for, and it felt more wonderful than Kate could have imagined.